# THE GALAXY WORLD CUP

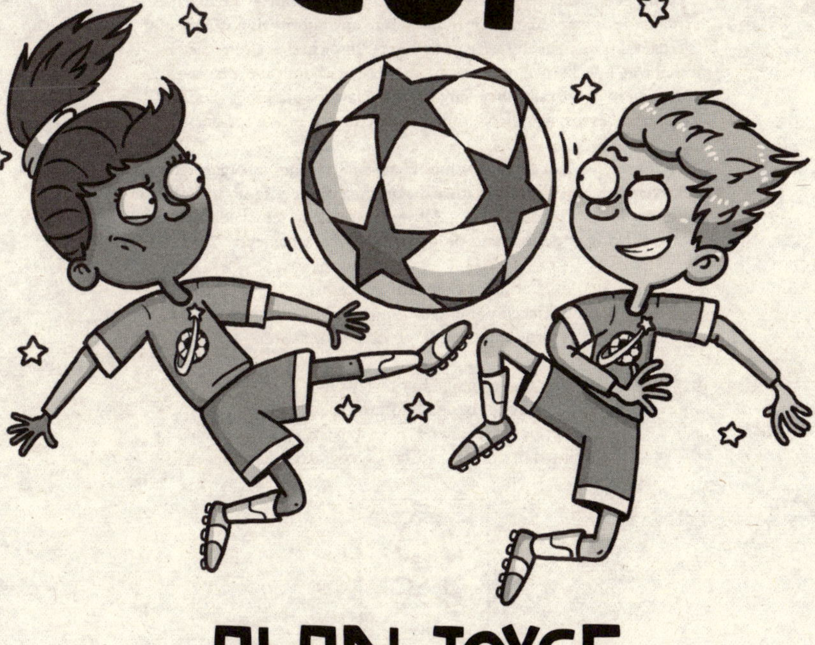

## ALAN JOYCE

2 PALMER STREET, FROME, SOMERSET, BA11 1DS

First published in the UK in 2026
Chicken House
2 Palmer Street
Frome, Somerset BA11 1DS
United Kingdom
www.chickenhousebooks.com

Chicken House/Scholastic Ireland, 89E Lagan Road, Dublin Industrial Estate, Glasnevin, Dublin D11 HP5F, Republic of Ireland

Text © Alan Joyce 2026
Illustration © Aleksei Bitskoff 2026

The moral rights of the author and illustrator have been asserted.

All rights reserved.
No part of this publication may be reproduced, transmitted, downloaded, decompiled, reverse engineered, used to train any artificial intelligence technologies, or stored in or introduced into any information storage and retrieval system, in any form or by any means, whether electronic or mechanical, now known or hereafter invented, without the express written permission of the publisher. Subject to EU law the publisher expressly reserves this work from the text and data mining exception.

This book is a work of fiction. Names, characters, businesses, organizations, places, events and incidents are either the product of the author's imagination or used in a fictitious manner. Any resemblance to actual persons, living or dead, events or locales is purely coincidental.

For safety or quality concerns:
UK: www.chickenhousebooks.com/productinformation
EU: www.scholastic.ie/productinformation

Cover design by Steve Wells
Interior design by Steve Wells
Typeset by Dorchester Typesetting Group Ltd
Printed in the UK by Clays, Elcograf S.p.A

1 3 5 7 9 10 8 6 4 2

A CIP catalogue record for this book is available from the British Library.

PB ISBN 978-1-917171-36-6
eISBN 978-1-917171-37-3

*This book is dedicated to the rest of my five-a-side team:*

*Lisa, Abbey, Ethan and Joel*

*XXX*

A short time ago in our galaxy far, far away, a speech was written by an alien named Gaux...

OUR GALAXY, THE MILKY WAY, IS APPROXIMATELY 100,000 LIGHT YEARS ACROSS AND CONTAINS WITHIN IT OVER ONE HUNDRED TRILLION FOOTBALLS. IT'S TRUE! FOOTBALL IS NOT ONLY THE MOST POPULAR SPORT ON PLANET EARTH, IT'S THE MOST POPULAR SPORT IN THE ENTIRE GALAXY. IT'S BUILT INTO THE VERY FABRIC OF TIME AND SPACE; PLANETS AREN'T JUST ROUND FOR NO REASON. WHENEVER A WORLD CONTAINING INTELLIGENT BEINGS BEGINS TO DEVELOP, THEY ALWAYS START WITH THE WHEEL, AND WITH FURTHER PROGRESS THEY EVENTUALLY ARRIVE AT THE FOOTBALL. AND WHEN THAT PLANET'S

FOOTBALLERS DEVELOP TO THE REQUIRED LEVEL OF FOOTBALLING ABILITY, WELL, THAT'S WHEN WE SHOW UP. EARTH HAS NOW REACHED THAT LEVEL, AND I AM HERE TO INVITE YOU TO PARTICIPATE IN THE GREATEST COMPETITION IN THE KNOWN UNIVERSE:

# THE GALAXY WORLD CUP

# CHAPTER ONE

On an outer spiral arm of the Milky Way galaxy, in the north-east of England, in the small town of Hebbrow, sat Nick Wilson, and he was very bored. He hated school, especially his, St Ernie's (the patron saint of boredom). At twelve years old, he found everything about it boring. The uniforms were boring (a dull, dark grey with a black-and-blue striped tie), the subjects and teachers were boring, even this sentence was boring.

Nick was what fellow Earthlings would describe as an ordinary schoolkid. His ink-blotched blazer sat on a scrawny body, topped off with a blonde-haired head full of hopes and daydreams.

The head of the school and part-time science teacher, Mrs Hawn, was droning on and on about something science-y, when Nick's thoughts turned to the window. It was so much better than science. Outside, Nick could go anywhere, or be anyone. A famous footballer? Or a hero, who saves the world? Anyone other than himself. He looked out at the main road. Cars were driving by. Nick wondered just how many red cars he could count. *Oh, there's one.*

'Earth to Mr Wilson,' said Mrs Hawn.

But Nick wasn't listening – the window had him. *That's six red cars in one minute – that has to be a record!*

'Mr Wilson!' screamed Mrs Hawn.

The window's spell was broken. Nick slowly turned around. The whole class was staring at him.

Lucas Marshall sat in front of him. The most popular kid in their class, their year – in fact, their entire school! The kids and teachers loved him and he definitely loved himself. He was tall, strong, athletic, and captain of the school's elite five-a-side football team, Ernie's United. He'd been on the books at Newcastle United since the age of seven. He was destined for the very top. Whereas Nick was destined to fail.

Lucas looked at Nick and held up his right hand to his forehead. With his thumb stuck out and index finger raised to form the letter 'L', he silently mouthed the word 'Loser'.

Nick didn't love Lucas Marshall and Lucas definitely had no love for him. Lucas found it fun to make Nick feel miserable. If only Nick had the courage to stand up to him.

But that Nick Wilson only existed outside the window, in his daydreams.

'Mr Wilson, you've finally decided to join us,' said Mrs Hawn. She reminded Nick of a flamingo, with her skinny frame, bright pink face and beady eyes. 'We are currently learning about the solar system. I'm fascinated to understand how looking out of the window helps with that?'

'I don't know,' said Nick.

'Exactly. That's because looking out of the

window doesn't help anybody.'

'He needs the practice, Miss,' said Lucas. 'For his work experience at the drive-through.'

The class broke out in laughter.

'OK, settle down,' said Mrs Hawn. 'Now, Mr Wilson, we're currently discussing the sixth planet from the sun – can you name it?'

'The planet?'

'Yes, the planet.'

'Erm . . . is it Pluto?'

The class laughed.

Mrs Hawn bit her lip. 'Pluto is no longer even a planet.'

'What? Why?' asked Nick.

'Can anyone inform Nick here as to why Pluto is not a planet?'

Eddie Chung, Nick's best and only friend, raised his hand. His wild Albert Einstein haircut matched his wild eyes. Everyone thought he looked like a cross between a mad scientist and just plain mad.

'Oh, this should be good,' said Mrs Hawn. 'Yes, Edward?'

'It was destroyed, Miss.'

'I'm sorry . . . what?'

'The planet – it was destroyed.' Eddie had seen one science fiction movie too many. Last summer he'd had a movie marathon at home, watching all the *Star Trek* and *Star Wars* movies back-to-back, without sleep. Nick thought his friend had never been the same since.

'And who destroyed it, Mr Chung?'

'The Empire, Miss, with their Death Star.'

The class erupted into fits of laughter.

'Get out, Chung,' said Mrs Hawn.

'What? I don't understand,' said Eddie.

'That's right, you don't. Now, out!'

Eddie got up and left the room, looking quite confused. Mrs Hawn turned back to Nick.

'So, Mr Wilson, why don't you look back out the window? Maybe the answer to the sixth planet lies out there.'

The class giggled.

Nick glanced out of the window. He looked over the main road, past the town's old community centre, which also doubled as the school's gym. He could see the park, and beyond that, Covington

Woods. Nick's eyes widened. Hovering above Covington Woods was a strange, silver, shimmering disc. The disc zipped down into the woods at lightning speed.

'Wilson, stop looking out of the window!' yelled Mrs Hawn.

'You told me to!'

'And you can stop with the answering back as well. I bet you don't do that at home, do you?'

'No.' He couldn't even if he wanted to. His parents had recently split up. Mrs Hawn didn't know that he went home to an empty house. His dad had moved out and his mum was always working. Each evening he'd sit alone in his room for hours on end.

'Exactly,' said Mrs Hawn.

'I don't do science at home either. Does that mean I can stop doing that as well?'

'Get out, Wilson.'

'What? I didn't do anything,' pleaded Nick.

'Precisely. Now, *out!*'

Nick left the room looking just as confused as Eddie.

\*

After the lesson, Mrs Hawn called them back into the classroom.

'What am I going to do with you two?' she said. 'You have so much potential, but you're wasting it by watching too many movies or staring out of the window and daydreaming your life away. Keep going down that road and you won't accomplish anything in this world.'

'I'm going to be an astronaut, Miss,' said Eddie. 'I'm going into space.'

'You do realize that watching sci-fi movies does not make you an astronaut, Edward? You have to actually study. You don't just suddenly end up in space.'

'It's hard to find time to study when it's just me and my grandma at home,' said Eddie. 'She's old. I have tons of chores to do.'

Nick had plenty of time to study, but no one at home to motivate him to do it.

'Well, then. I think a small stint in detention might set you both back on the right road. That extra study time's exactly what you both need.'

She sent them on their way with a week's detention each.

As they plodded off towards their next lesson, Nick caught a glimpse of Covington Woods through a window. He told Eddie all about the strange disc.

Eddie was convinced it was aliens. 'We have to go to the woods, now!'

'We can't go now, we're in enough trouble already. Plus, we've got double history.'

'If that UFO turns out to be space invaders,' said Eddie, 'we're the ones who'll be history.'

# CHAPTER TWO

Nick and Eddie walked into detention to find no teacher present, and two other pupils already there: Phil Beatty and Mia Welsh.

Phil was a year older than Nick. His skinny, gangly frame put him at least a foot taller too.

Mia Welsh was in Nick's year. She was small, but made up for it in anger. Rumour had it she had a tattoo on her upper left arm: a list of all the people's noses she'd bitten. From behind her long locks of brown hair, she snarled at Eddie and flashed Nick a mean look. Nick quickly looked away.

'I hope Mrs Hawn isn't taking detention,' said Nick.

'Hey, are we still going to the woods after school, then?' said Eddie.

'Yeah, shh!' hissed Nick.

'Why "shh"? What's in the woods?' asked Phil.

'Nick saw a spaceship land there.'

Mia laughed. 'Don't be daft.'

'He did! It's probably from Pluto. They need to conquer us to find somewhere new to live, since it's been destroyed.'

'Shut up.' Nick punched Eddie's arm.

'Ouch! That hurt,' said Eddie, rubbing at the sore spot. 'Anyway, we're going to the woods to check it out.'

'Is this detention?' said a small squeaky voice. Everyone looked at the door to see another kid. Thin as an exclamation mark, he looked like he'd snap in the breeze.

'What's your name?' asked Nick.

He sneezed, then squeaked, 'It's Sanjay Singh, but my friends call me the Singhster.'

'The Singhster,' said Eddie. 'I like it. I'm Eddie

and that's Nick – it's short for "he nicked all the test answers, that's why he's here".'

'No, it isn't,' said Nick.

'You don't look like you belong in detention,' said Phil. 'What did you do?'

'I forgot to bring my homework in,' said Sanjay.

'Classic mistake,' said Eddie. 'You've got to be more inventive, like, it was eaten by my nana or something.'

'But she's got no teeth,' Sanjay said, and sneezed again.

'Wait,' said Nick, 'are you Singhster456, who posts all the top gaming tips on the school's website?'

'I used to be,' said Sanjay, 'but my parents said it was interfering with my schoolwork.'

Judging by the detention, they weren't wrong, thought Nick.

'They got rid of my computer, said I needed to get out of my room more often.'

'I don't think detention counts,' said Eddie.

'Trust me, it does,' said Phil. 'I actually don't mind detention – anything that gets me away from that shop.'

Phil's parents ran a local convenience store, and his access to an endless supply of sweets was legendary around the playground. He'd often bring in a backpack full of them to sell to the other kids at break time, at expensive prices. Unfortunately, this little money-maker had been rumbled by Mr Anders, and Phil had been given two weeks' detention. 'And don't get me started on my younger brother and sister,' he continued. 'They have no respect for my privacy. The sooner I've left home, the better.'

'Will you all shut up?' said Mia. 'I like peace and quiet in detention, I don't want to hear you lot babbling on.'

'Sorry,' said Sanjay.

Nick looked at Mia. 'Why are you here?'

'Me?' said Mia. 'Well, somebody asked me a question, so I bit his nose off.'

Nick gulped and took a step back. 'I was only asking.'

'This is just like that old film,' said Phil.

'Yeah, *Guardians of the Galaxy*,' said Eddie.

'*How?*' said Nick. 'How is it like *Guardians of*

*the Galaxy?*'

'Well, we're like the crew, aren't we?'

'No,' said Nick, shaking his head.

Sanjay sneezed and wiped his nose with the arm of his blazer.

Phil opened his backpack. 'Does anybody want to buy any sweets?'

Mia slammed her hands down on her desk. 'No. Now be quiet!'

'All of you be quiet.' Mr Barton marched into the classroom, carrying an enormous gym bag. He was the school's PE teacher. He dropped the bag and did a few warm-up stretches, his muscles bulging beneath his bright red tracksuit.

'OK, is this it?' said Mr Barton. He counted round the room. 'Five, perfect! Follow me!' He grabbed his bag and marched back out of the room.

They followed him out of the classroom, then out of the school and across the main road and into the old community centre.

You could smell the old gym before you actually got there. Its stink was legendary. They held their noses and followed Mr Barton in. The only thing left inside was the five-a-side pitch. Everything else, from the basketball hoops to the cricket nets, had either worn away or been stolen. But as Nick's dad would often say, the local council had better things to spend its money on. Like massive pay rises for the town councillors.

They marched on to the football playing area. At the other end of the gym, kitted out in their red training bibs, were Lucas Marshall and his Ernie's United teammates. They spotted Nick and the others and burst into laughter.

Mr Barton dumped his bag on the centre circle. 'You'll each find a shirt and shorts in there. Quickly get changed and be back on the pitch in five minutes. My team needs shooting practice, and you're it.'

The stench coming from the bag made the gym smell positively fragrant.

'Have these shirts been washed, sir?' asked Nick.

'They will be after you lot have used them. Now go and get changed.'

They each reluctantly dipped their hands into

the bag and took out a shirt and pair of shorts. Nick's shirt was the only one with long sleeves.

Mia sniffed hers. 'I'm not wearing those, no way.'

'Call it extra punishment, Miss Welsh,' said Mr Barton. 'And if you don't wear it, you'll be letting the whole team down, so you'll all be on detention for the rest of your life.'

'That's not fair,' said Nick.

'Life's not fair. Get used to it,' said Mr Barton. He turned and walked over to join the other team.

Sanjay sniffed his top and sneezed. 'I've got a cold. I don't smell a thing.'

'Good for you,' said Mia. 'I'm not wearing it.'

Nick spoke up: 'Mia, it's only for an hour or so, come on, do it for the team.'

'What team? I don't even know you people.'

Eddie looked hurt. 'I'm Eddie, we met in the detention room. Don't say you've forgotten already?'

Mia shook her head. Nick could tell she was not impressed with them, her teammates, all of whom looked more . . . pathetic, than athletic: Eddie, who was one planet short of a solar system; Phil, more interested in selling sweets than playing sweet;

Sanjay, who looked lost without his computer; and himself, ordinary loser Nick Wilson.

'*Fine!* I'll do it, but not for you lot, I'm doing it for me.'

'There's no "me" in team,' said Eddie. 'Oh wait, hang on . . .'

'And,' said Mia, 'I want your long-sleeved top.' She grabbed the top off Nick and threw him hers. She stormed off towards the girls' changing room.

Eddie shook his head. 'I just don't understand girls.'

'Or physics, or maths, or anything,' chuckled Nick, as they all headed to the boys' changing room.

The football strips were the school's own colours, grey shorts with a black-and-blue striped top. Eddie noticed they had famous footballers' names printed on the back.

'Wait, I wanna be Messi.' He grabbed the top off Sanjay and gave him his Haaland shirt.

Nick already had his top on. 'Who am I?'

'You're Cristiano Ronaldo,' said Eddie.

'I'm Mbappé,' said Phil. 'Who's he?'

'Frenchman,' said Sanjay. 'He's a striker.'

'That sounds like running around. I'll play in goal,' said Phil. 'Who's Haaland then?'

'I'm a towering Norwegian goal machine, who plays for Man City,' said the tiny Sanjay Singh.

'I wonder who Mia got?' said Eddie.

'Let's find out,' said Nick, leading them out of the changing room and back into the stinky hall.

Mia was waiting for them, next to their goal. Eddie ran over and asked whose name she'd got on her shirt.

'Morgan,' said Mia.

Eddie looked at Sanjay for an explanation. 'Morgan,' said Sanjay, 'captained Leicester City to the Premier League title in the 2015/16 season.'

'No,' said Mia, 'women play football as well, you know. I'm Alex Morgan – she played for the USA and the San Diego Wave.'

'Now,' said Mr Barton, 'whichever side loses, they'll be doing laps of the park as a punishment.' He blew his whistle and the teams lined up. On one side of the gym, St Ernie's United, and on the other, the Detention Dynamite: Nick/Ronaldo,

Mia/Morgan, Eddie/Messi, Sanjay/Haaland and Phil/Mbappé. They were kitted up and ready to play – well, maybe not *ready*.

Nick looked at his teammates. 'Do any of you actually know how to play football?'

'I'm more of a cricket man,' said Phil. 'But my parents' shop sells the Panini football stickers. I can get you a pack in school, with only a fifteen per cent mark-up value.'

'I've seen the movie *Space Jam*,' said Eddie.

'That's basketball, Eddie,' replied Nick. 'How about you, Sanjay?'

Sanjay wiggled his fingers. 'These are deadly weapons in the gaming world, I'm amazing at FIFA on the Xbox. Just no good in the real world.'

Nick looked at Mia. 'Please say you play?'

Mia grinned. 'I've got five older brothers. I've been forced to play footy since birth.'

'Great,' said Nick. 'If any of you get the ball, pass to Mia. Let's try and keep the score down to a respectable level.'

Phil pulled on his goalkeeper gloves. 'Don't worry, Nick, I'm an expert wicket keeper. These hands are like an impenetrable wall, nothing gets past them, I could stop . . .'

'One–nil!' screamed Lucas, as he ran away from the goal.

'What?' Phil looked behind himself to see the ball nestled in the bottom left corner. 'I didn't even know we'd kicked off?'

'We weren't ready!' hollered Mia.

'Boo-hoo,' said Lucas.

Mia and Nick kicked off from the centre circle and the match restarted. The Detention Dynamite were all over the place. There was no teamwork, no communication, no nothing.

Mia had the ball when one of the Ernie's United players came from behind her and stole it away. She angrily turned on her teammates. 'You're supposed to tell me if there's a man on!'

'A man on what?' said Nick.

'A man on me!'

'He wasn't on you, he came in, like, from behind.'

Mia shook her head.

Nick's stomach sank. His confidence, already

low, was shrinking with every attempted kick or pass. Ernie's United were running riot. They were slick passers of the ball; they all knew their positions and were constantly on the attack. It wasn't long before more goals were flying in.

'Hey, Mia,' said Eddie. 'Any chance you could pass the ball now and then? You're hogging it.'

'What for? You lot are rubbish.'

'Eddie's right,' said Nick. 'We need to work more as a team.'

Mia laughed. 'You've got more chance of us doing our homework.'

Ernie's United were on the offensive once more. Nick looked back towards his own goal and couldn't believe his eyes. Phil wasn't there. He'd moved to the side of the pitch and was tucking into a packet of beef crisps.

'What are you doing? You're the keeper!'

'I was just a bit peckish . . . It's boring being in goal. Reminds me of being stuck behind the shop counter all day.'

'Boring? The ball's flying past you every three seconds, you're the busiest player on our team! I thought you said nothing gets past you – did you mean *everything* gets past you?' said Nick.

'Whoa, you need to calm down,' said Phil. 'This is just a friendly.'

The match restarted. Eddie had the ball.

'One, two?' suggested Nick.

'Three, four?' replied a confused Eddie. Lucas barged Eddie off the ball and passed to a teammate up the pitch.

Nick slapped his own forehead in despair. 'It means you pass the ball to me for a one, two. You pass the ball, then move and I pass it back.'

'Why didn't you just say, "me, you", then?' said Eddie.

Mr Barton blew his whistle. 'That's six–nil. You people couldn't pass salt at the dinner table. You just aren't team players.'

'Salt is bad for you,' said Sanjay.

'Don't answer back, boy.'

Another twenty-five minutes later and Phil had retrieved the ball from his net a further sixteen times.

'Twenty-two–nil, a turkey shoot,' said Mr Barton.

'Well, at least you've got six—'

'We did? I thought we'd scored none,' said Eddie.

'You didn't let me finish,' said Mr Barton. 'At least you've got six laps of the park to do. Gives you time to reflect on where the game went wrong.' He blew his whistle. 'Go!'

Lucas and the rest of Ernie's United pointed and laughed. 'Bye, losers!'

Sore, tired and defeated, the Detention Dynamite trudged their way out of the gym, heading for the park. Little did they know that their lives were about to change, for ever.

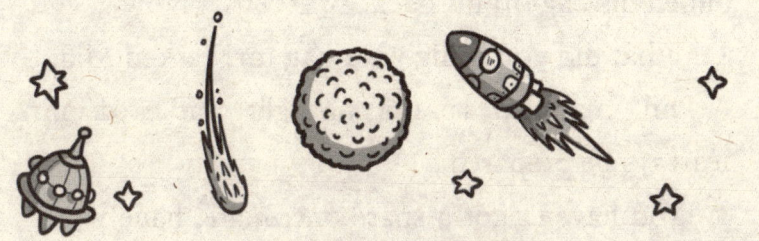

# CHAPTER THREE

The park was quiet at this time of day. The only people Nick could see were an elderly couple feeding the ducks on the small murky lake. The team slowly jogged past them.

'I haven't run this far since I chased after that ice-cream van last summer,' said Eddie.

Nick suddenly stopped. Everyone piled into the back of him.

'Why are we running, anyway?' said Nick. 'Nobody's here, Mr Barton's not even watching... We could just wait ten minutes and say we've done it.'

'I'm with Nick on this,' said Phil, panting. He pulled his bag off his back.

'What did you bring your bag for?' asked Mia.

Phil unzipped it and brought out a drink. 'Always be prepared.'

'You haven't got a spare one, mate, have you?' asked Eddie.

'Of course, if you have a spare two quid.'

'What? We're teammates!'

'Yeah, but I'm saving up for a trip to the cricket world cup. "Beatty saves"; it's my mantra.'

'You didn't do much saving when you were in goal,' said Nick.

'What's a mantra?' asked Sanjay.

'It's who Godzilla usually fights with,' said Eddie.

'So, no cash, no drink,' said Phil.

'Here.' Sanjay handed over a ten-pound note, which he'd pulled from his sock. 'Drinks for everyone.'

Eddie wrapped his arm around Sanjay. 'The Singhster, what a guy.'

Phil took the money and gave everyone a can of pop. His bag seemed capable of storing an endless number of treats. They were all enjoying their drinks when a strange noise behind them caused them to stop. They slowly turned around to face Covington Woods.

The woods had always seemed scary to Nick. As a young child, he'd imagined that wolves and witches lived there, plotting to steal and eat children. Even now, with the sun still up, the woods looked menacing, as if evil lurked behind every tree trunk. The strange clunking noise came again.

'It's the aliens,' said Eddie.

'Don't be stupid,' said Mia. 'It's probably an owl.' Even as she said it, the expression on her face suggested that she knew this was no owl.

'No . . . Could be a woodpecker though,' said Phil.

Nick closed his eyes and whispered to himself, 'It's not wolves or witches.'

'What do you think, Sanjay?' asked Eddie.

Sanjay finished his can of pop and burped. 'I think this pop's lovely.'

A green glowing light shot back and forth across the trees.

Eddie's eyes lit up. 'OK, I don't care if it's alien owls, alien woodpeckers or alien wolves and witches, it's *definitely* aliens. I've waited my whole life for this. I'm going into the woods.' Eddie took a step towards the park's fence. 'Who's coming with me?' Nobody moved.

'Come on!' said Eddie. 'We're a team. I can't go on my own – there's no "I" in team.'

'But there is an "I" in idiot,' said Nick.

'Two, actually,' added Phil.

Sanjay sneezed and stepped forward. 'Think of all that alien technology. I'll go.'

'Told you,' said Phil.

'Come on, Mia, if you don't think it's aliens, what have you got to be scared of?'

Mia flashed Eddie an evil stare. 'I'm not scared!' She stepped forward.

'Nick?' said Eddie.

Nick didn't want to look frightened in front of Mia, so he stepped forward as well.

Phil sighed. 'Oh, *cheese and onion crisps*. I can't go back alone, can I?' He reluctantly joined the others.

They worked their way along the park fence till they found an opening. One by one, they squeezed through into the woods.

They carried on through the trees and bushes. Fifty metres in, it felt like a whole new world: insects, birds, flowers . . . You could imagine you were in the deepest, darkest rainforest on the other side of the planet.

'I haven't been this far into the woods since I was chased by that ice-cream van last summer,' said Eddie.

Mia rolled her eyes.

'Don't worry,' said Nick. 'You get used to him.'

'Hopefully not,' said Mia.

Nick smiled. 'So,' he said, 'what were you really in detention for?'

'I chucked a rock through the art department window.'

The art department window was one of Nick's favourites: you could see the whole school field through it. 'That was you? Why?'

Mia shrugged her shoulders. 'Seemed like a good idea at the time.'

Eddie pointed to the right. 'The light came from over there.'

They continued on, eventually stumbling out into a clearing.

'There's nothing here,' said Nick.

'You're good at stating the obvious, aren't you?' said Mia.

But Nick was right: the clearing was empty. It was circular in shape, with weather-worn grass and some old sweet wrappers, but there was nothing out of the ordinary, and definitely no aliens.

'What a waste of time,' Mia added.

'Are you always angry, or do you have, like, a week off in June?' asked Eddie. Mia moved towards Eddie, her fists at the ready. Clearly not wanting to end up on her tattooed list of names, Eddie jumped back into the clearing and was knocked out cold by the fresh air. He landed on the grass with a thud.

Mia held up her hands. 'I never touched him, I swear.'

Nick bent down and patted him on the cheek. 'Eddie, you OK?'

As Nick continued to pat his cheek, Eddie slowly came round. His eyes flickered. 'I'll have a 99 and a Cornetto, erm . . . What? Where am I?'

'You fell down.'

'No, he didn't,' said Phil. 'Look!'

Sanjay had stepped into the clearing and was pushing against something that wasn't there. Either Sanjay was the world's best mime artist, or there was an enormous invisible object in front of him.

'Sanjay's the world's best mime artist!' yelled Eddie.

Nick felt along the invisible barrier, its cold surface vibrating under his touch. Mia joined them, pushing against the nothing. It was solid.

'What is going on?' asked Phil, opening another bag of crisps.

Meanwhile . . . inside the spacecraft (which was called *Messenger*), an alien named Gaux and his humanoid robot, Nauton, stared at the main deck monitor screen.

'It can't be,' said Gaux. Gaux was what Earthlings would describe as a classic alien. A green-skinned, beanpole body resting on four legs, with long fingers attached to thin, muscleless arms, topped off with a large oval head.

Buttons beeped on Nauton's chest. 'It's them, sir, I'm telling you.' His voice sounded like an English butler. Nauton was old, rusty and had been repaired so many times over the years, his different parts now resembled a scarecrow robot (used to frighten away viruses). On the plus side, he was still capable of eleven million computations per second. How correct those computations were was anyone's guess, least of all Nauton's. 'Check their shirts, sir.' The screen showed the backs of each of the kids: Ronaldo, Messi, Morgan, Haaland and Mbappé.

'How did they know we were coming?'

'Beats me, but my databanks show these are some of the world's best. Especially Ronaldo and Messi.'

'Yes, I know all about Ronaldo and Messi. I just can't believe they knew where to find us! We landed here by accident. I thought it was going to take days to track them down.'

'Maybe it was just an amazing coincidence, sir.'

'Well, open the hatch and lower the gangplank – it's time to deliver my speech.'

Back outside, and the team were talking over what to do next.

'It's got to be the UFO!' said Nick.

'This is gonna make us famous,' said Eddie. 'We'll be on every news website!'

'No, we won't,' said Phil. 'The American government will cover it up.'

'He's right,' said Sanjay.

'They'll put it in Area 51,' added Nick.

'Listen,' said Eddie, 'forget the American government. We go straight on the internet, blow this whole thing wide open.'

'But we don't even know what this is,' said Mia.

'*Aliens!* How many times do I have to say it?' said Eddie.

'It might not be,' said Phil.

'It's not . . . *woodpeckers*, is it?' screamed Eddie.

Their conversation was interrupted by a large hissing noise. Everyone jumped back in surprise as a huge metal door appeared. Slowly, it tilted forward all the way to the ground, creating a gangplank. Smoke billowed from the opening, blocking the inside view. The team gaped with open mouths as a rusty humanoid robot clanked down the gangplank.

Nick thought the sight of a being from another world was scarier than all the imagined wolves and witches put together. He struggled not to pee in his shorts.

Eddie was stunned. 'The films were right; aliens exist!'

Mia clenched her fists. 'If they've come to take over, I'm ready for the fight.'

'Do you think they'd be interested in buying some sweets?' asked Phil.

'I wonder what kind of operating system they have?' said Sanjay. Who then sneezed.

Nauton raised his metal hand. 'Greetings, Earth people . . .' But that was as far as he got. Gaux fired his stun gun at the team, knocking them unconscious.

'What happened to the *speech*?' asked Nauton.

Gaux nervously smiled. 'My butterflies got the best of me. I get really nervous at public speaking. Thought it was best to just do it the old-fashioned way and abduct them. I'll explain everything when they're on board and we're off into hyperspace.'

'Works for me,' said Nauton. He sent a message to the ship's computer, activating the vessel's tractor beam. One by one, the football team members floated up the gangplank and into the ship's belly. Nauton and Gaux followed, and the gangplank closed behind them.

Four well-fed ducks watched in awe as a strange, metallic disc-like object floated up and out of Covington Woods, before shooting off at lightning speed.

Twenty-eight seconds later, and the ship had left Earth's atmosphere, and was heading for the distant stars.

# CHAPTER FOUR

Nick was having the strangest of dreams. An alien killer robot was blasting a ray gun in the woods, killing wolves and witches. Mia stood by his side. The killer robot aimed the gun at Mia. She turned to Nick, opened her mouth and bit his nose . . .

Nick's eyes opened and his nightmare didn't disappear. In fact, it was on the other side of the room, talking to an alien. He blinked to make sure his eyes were not deceiving him. They weren't. On the other side of this strange circular chamber, having a chat with the killer robot, was an alien.

For once in his life, Eddie had been right. This was an alien invasion!

Nick tried to move, but found his arms and legs were strapped to the table he was lying on.

'Where are you taking us?' he yelled.

The alien turned, and scuttled over to Nick on his four stumpy legs. He pressed a button on his hand tablet and Nick's table tilted upright so he looked like he was standing. He scanned the room and saw the others were strapped to tables, too. Nick looked back at the alien and it began to speak.

'Whoa, slow down, I can't understand a single word you're saying,' said Nick. He was trying hard not to cry.

Gaux frowned. 'What's up with Ronaldo? He looks a bit wimpy to me. In fact, all of them seem a bit puny.'

'The Galactic Union of Football Federations says that this planet has reached the required footballing level, sir,' said Nauton.

'What do the GUFF know about football?

They're all just a bunch of overpaid Quillians. Especially their leader, Squirmo. He probably hasn't kicked a ball in his entire life.'

'Well, that's true, sir,' said Nauton. 'Squirmo, like all the Quillians, has no legs. He's never played football. I believe the Quillian national sport is mind-control chess.'

Gaux looked again at the whimpering Ronaldo. 'Are you sure it's definitely them?'

Nauton's databanks beeped and twirled. 'The players' shirts say so: their names are right there on the back. And look.' Nauton pointed to the front of Nick's strip. 'It says "E United". That must be their team name, Earth United. It's definitely them, sir. This is Cristiano Ronaldo, the highest-scoring international player ever!'

'Stop. I know who they all are,' said Gaux. 'The resistance wouldn't have fixed it for me to be head coach if I didn't know what I was doing. Now, go and sort this language barrier out – I've a team to greet.'

Nauton left the chamber.

*

Nick turned his head to see Eddie waking up and could tell all of Eddie's wildest dreams had come true: he was in space, he was in a spaceship, and standing next to him was an alien. The alien moved to a monitor on the far side of the chamber and tapped on the screen with its long, bony fingers.

'It's an alien! I was right!' whispered Eddie.

'I know,' whispered Nick. 'I think it's the first time ever. Where do you think they're taking us?'

'Probably to the command ship. It's where they'll interrogate us.'

'Interrogate us?' gulped Sanjay, who was now awake.

'Stop scaring him, Eddie,' said Nick. 'This isn't science fiction, this is science fact.'

'Oh, you mean like *Star Trek*.'

Phil's eyes opened. 'Oh, no . . . This doesn't look like Covington Woods.'

'You're right there – we're currently hurtling through outer space,' said Nick.

Phil looked stricken. 'Oh, *Fry's Chocolate Cream*. I suffer from terrible travel sickness, I get ill just playing Risk.' As if on cue, his stomach rumbled.

Nick looked at Mia, who was still knocked out. She looked different when she was sleeping – peaceful, even.

The killer robot came back in, carrying a tray with five syringes on it. Eddie's eyes widened. 'Who knows what those injections do!' Eddie shook with fear, then he fainted.

Beads of sweat broke out on Nick's forehead as the killer robot menacingly approached. Nick wriggled, but it was no use. The killer robot picked up one of the syringes, found a vein on Nick's hand and sank the needle in. Nick closed his eyes, gritted his teeth and waited for the pain, the drowsiness, or at least something.

Nothing happened. Opening his eyes once more, he found that the smiling green alien was stood in front of him. The robot was moving around the room, giving a syringe to each of Nick's teammates.

'OK,' said the alien, 'the universal translator should be taking effect by now. Can – you – understand – me?'

'Yes!' said a shocked Nick. 'I do understand you, but I don't understand how.'

The alien chuckled. 'A simple injection of a nano-translator. It means you can now understand any language in the universe.'

'Any language?' asked Nick.

The alien nodded.

'For how long?'

'For ever.'

'Wow, that's gonna come in handy on the French oral exam!'

The alien smiled and said, 'My name is Gaux. And my robot companion is Nauton.'

'So, where are you taking us?' asked Nick.

Gaux began to speak, but Nick had noticed something else over the alien's left shoulder . . . There was a window! Nick could see stars, and a planet, and the planet was *red*! He wondered how many red planets he could count.

Gaux clicked his three fingers in front of Nick's face. 'Excuse me.'

The window's spell was broken, and Nick looked back at Gaux. 'Yes?'

'Were you looking out of the window?' asked Gaux.

'Yes. Isn't that Mars?'

'Did you hear anything I said?'

'Get these things off me! I'm gonna kill you all!'

Looked like Mia was awake.

Gaux looked at Nauton. 'Morgan looks angry, Nauton. Will the straps hold?'

Nauton moved away from Mia. 'My databanks say eighty-seven per cent sure they will.'

Mia was getting angrier by the second. Nauton beeped. 'Now thirty-seven per cent.'

'Please, calm down,' begged Gaux.

Mia was having none of it. 'I'm gonna bite your noses off!'

'Twenty-three per cent, sir,' said a nervous Nauton.

'Maybe the translator's broken and she doesn't understand our language?' suggested Gaux.

'I understand your language all right!' screamed Mia. 'Now understand mine: !!!**£$%$**!!!' Words flew out of Mia's mouth that even the universal translator couldn't interpret.

Sanjay sneezed, sending snot all over Nauton.

Phil was turning green. 'I'm travel sick!'

Eddie was still out cold, and Nick had gone back to looking out of the window.

Gaux had had enough. He pulled out his stun gun and sent a blast into the ceiling.

Nick looked away from the window, Mia stopped yelling, Sanjay ceased sneezing, Phil was still ill, and Eddie woke up.

'You people are the worst,' said Gaux. 'As representatives of Planet Earth, I expected much better.'

'*Representatives?*' said Nick. 'You *abducted* us – we had no choice!'

'He's got a point there, sir,' said Nauton.

'But you came to meet the ship,' said Gaux. 'You knew we were there.'

All the teammates began to shout out at Gaux all at once.

'I can't understand when you're all talking at the same time,' said Gaux. It didn't matter, they all continued to shout out together. Gaux pulled out his gun and fired once more. 'Silence! If you all just shut up for a minute, I'll explain everything.'

Everyone looked at the gun and fell silent. 'Good,' said Gaux. 'First, I apologize for the abduction. That was my fault, I get nervous about doing speeches. Second . . .'

A light flashed on Nauton's chest plate. 'We're coming up on the wormhole, sir.'

'Don't forget to dump our rubbish; you know it slows down wormhole travel,' said Gaux.

'Already done, sir,' said Nauton.

'Wormhole?' said Nick. 'Where are you taking us?'

'We'll be travelling to the other side of the galaxy, to a planet called Bigpu.'

There was a moment's silence, then all the teammates burst out laughing.

'What's so funny?' asked Gaux.

Nauton leant over to Gaux. 'In their primitive language, sir, it's what they usually have every morning, to get rid of excess waste.'

'OK, calm down,' said Gaux. 'There's no need to be rude, especially when your planet is only named after a bit of mud. So, we'll be going to Bigpu.'

Everyone burst out laughing again.

'This is ridiculous,' said Gaux. 'OK, from now on I won't say the whole planet's name, I'll just call it Big-P.'

The team burst out laughing even louder.

'What have I said now?'

Nauton leant over and explained it to Gaux.

'OK, never mind! We're going to another planet – it's where the Galactic Union of Football Federations, or GUFF, have their HQ. It's also where this year's Galaxy World Cup will be held. Your world has now met the required footballing status, and you've been invited as representatives of Planet Earth.'

'We enter the wormhole in eight seconds, sir,' said Nauton.

'We're being taken to the other side of the galaxy to watch a football game?' said a bemused Nick.

'Watch?' said Gaux. 'No, no, you've misunderstood – you're playing in it.'

Before the team had a chance to reply, the ship entered the wormhole.

# CHAPTER FIVE

Interstellar wormhole travel is considerably more difficult than say, a journey from Leeds to London. One, there are no roads, and two, you must bend the very fabric of space and time. Lucky for us, then, that a race of builders called the Markasians worked out how to do it. You simply pick two places in the universe you wish to travel between, then fold the universe like a piece of paper, so that the two match up. Then, you stick a size 26 pencil through the universe, harnessing the power of a nearby star, and Bob's your uncle, you have a wormhole.

One second into the journey and the ship bent with time and space. Everyone inside flexed and warped with it.

Nick noticed the ship's window was now infinite. Sanjay thought the wormhole looked like the Rainbow Road from Mario Kart mixed with the Hebbrow High Street underpass. It was 'looc' (cool, warped in time and space). Mia wanted to bite off the wormhole's nose. Eddie's hair flattened and parted itself for the first time in history. Phil was not well and two seconds later he vomited. His vomit spun around the chamber and felt sick itself. Phil's vomit then vomited.

The whole journey through the wormhole took precisely seven seconds, or three hours in British Rail time.

'That was excellent,' said Sanjay, who then sneezed.

Phil was covered in vomit. Eddie was covered in Phil's vomit's vomit. Mia was ready to kill the entire universe and Nick had counted sixty-four red planets and two burgundy ones.

Gaux swayed uneasily on his four legs. 'You

may all be suffering from a slight space-lag.'

'Get these restraints off me and you'll be the one suffering,' growled Mia.

'So let me get this right, you abducted us to play in a galactic football tournament?' asked Nick.

'Correct,' said Gaux. 'Thirty-two representatives from across the Milky Way compete in the ultimate five-a-side competition to see who wins the Galaxy World Cup. Your planet has been invited as this year's wildcard entry. It's an enormous honour.'

Sanjay looked at Nauton. 'Who are we playing, robot?'

Lights flashed on Nauton's chest. 'I believe, sir, your first match is against the Zzllontis.'

'Perfect,' said Gaux, smiling. 'The Zzllontis aren't very good, you'll easily beat them.'

'I still don't understand why you've brought us?' asked Nick.

'Because you're the best team on Planet Earth.'

Eddie burst out laughing.

'There's no need to be modest, Messi,' said Gaux. 'We've all read your football statistics.'

'*Messi?*' said a confused Nick. 'Wait, hang on!'

'No, you hang on, Ronaldo,' said Gaux, 'we've got a lot to do before the first match. Now, as you're the oldest you will be the Earth's team captain. I've been appointed head coach and could I just say, it's an absolute privilege to manage such fine footballers as yourselves. Messi, Ronaldo, Morgan, Mbappé and Haaland. The greatest players of Planet Earth . . . I know we're going to win this thing.'

A buzzer went off on Nauton's head. 'Sir, we're approaching Bigpu.'

'Excuse me, I must go and land the ship.'

Gaux headed out of the chamber, quickly followed by Nauton.

'They think that we're . . .'

Nick interrupted Eddie. 'I know what they think, Eddie.'

'We're gonna get hammered,' said Mia.

'This is going to be great,' said Sanjay.

'No, it isn't,' said Nick. 'What do you say, Phil?'

Phil opened his mouth and vomited some more down his chin.

'That about sums it up.'

'Yep,' said Eddie. 'When they find out we're not the footballers, we'll not only be *on* Bigpu, we'll be deep *in* it. You can forget about being interrogated, it'll be a straight vaporization.'

'We'll have to lie,' said Nick.

'What?' came the teammates' reply.

'They think we're the Earth's best footballers, why tell them any different? We'll just pretend to be Messi and Ronaldo.'

'Won't they find out the minute the first match kicks off?' said Eddie.

'Oh, *shut up*, Eddie,' said Nick. 'This is all your fault.'

'Me? How?'

'If we hadn't followed you into the woods, none of this would've happened.'

'Well, if you hadn't seen the spaceship, I wouldn't have wanted to go in the woods, so it's your fault.'

'No, it isn't.'

'It is!'

'Isn't!'

'Shut up!' yelled Mia. 'Here's what we're gonna do: we're gonna stick with Nick's plan because that keeps us alive a little bit longer. We'll deal with the first match when we get to it, so from now on we call each other by our football names, agreed?'

The new Ronaldo, Messi, Haaland and Mbappé all agreed with the new Morgan.

# CHAPTER SIX

Gaux piloted the ship down for their arrival at the spaceport, in the capital city of Oloo. The spaceport was one enormous glass dome, the size of the Isle of Wight. Ships were blasting off, but even more were landing. This was the busiest spaceport in the entire Milky Way, with over 300 billion aliens passing through it per year.

The metallic ties holding the team to the tables slid back. They were now free.

'Let's make a run for it,' said Eddie.

'I've done my quota of running for this month,' said Phil, as he wiped the sick from his chin.

'Where exactly are we going to run to?' said Nick. 'We're on an alien world on the other side of the galaxy.'

'Get me to the cockpit,' said Sanjay. 'I've clocked more space games than I can count. I'm pretty sure I could fly us out of here.'

'Yeah, but you'd need to get past the robot and laser-gun-holding alien first,' said Nick.

'Stick to the plan,' said Mia. 'We play along for now.'

Nauton arrived and led them all out of the chamber, down the gangplank and into the spaceport. Eddie began to giggle uncontrollably. Aliens were everywhere. They were coming, going, sliding, gliding and everything. There were green ones, blue ones, black, gold, shinarton and browlo (colours not yet available on Earth) ones. This was close encounters of the thousandth kind.

'We are definitely not alone in the universe,' said Nick. Mia looked at him. 'I'm stating the obvious again, aren't I?'

Mia nodded.

From the spaceport's domed ceiling hung

gigantic banners displaying the Galaxy World Cup's greatest players. The majority of which featured one particular player.

'Who's that?' asked Nick.

'That is the GOAT,' said Gaux.

'Goat?' replied Mia. 'He looks like a crocodile to me.'

'No, he's an alligator,' said Phil.

'Crocodile!'

'Alligator!'

'Actually,' said Gaux, 'you're both correct. That is Clawtic. He's the Bigpuvian captain and like all Bigpuvians, he is an allidile, a cross between a crocodile and an alligator.'

'I thought you said he was a goat,' said Eddie.

'No, I said he's *the* GOAT. Greatest-Of-All-Time. Nobody's as good as Clawtic.'

'I think Pelé might have something to say about that,' said Eddie.

'Who's he?' said Gaux.

'My auntie's prize-winning goat. Nobody eats grass like Pelé.'

Gaux shook his head.

'I hope he's not as tall and wide as he is in the banner . . . We wouldn't stand a chance,' said Sanjay.

'Yeah, and if he's as good as you say he is, maybe we should just go home now?' said Mia.

*If only*, thought Nick.

Gaux ignored Mia's remark and led the team over to the arrivals desk. Sitting behind it was a star-shaped orange creature with twelve tentacles, who introduced itself as Bly. Bly's face was in the centre of its body and was small but cheerful. Each of Bly's tentacles was busy at work, typing on computers or stamping bits of paper.

'State the nature of your visit?' said Bly.

Gaux puffed out his chest. 'This is the football team from Planet Earth, here to compete in the Galaxy World Cup.'

'Earth? Never heard of it,' said Bly, as it stretched out a tentacle. 'OK, hand over your passports.'

Gaux handed over his and Nauton's passports. He turned to look at Nick.

'What? We don't have them. Abducted, remember?'

Gaux turned back to face Bly. 'Erm, well you see, we left Earth in a bit of a hurry . . . They seem to have forgotten theirs.'

'We get aliens trying that one all the time – not gonna wash, mate. I mean, how do I know they're who they say they are? They could be anybody.'

Nick gulped.

Nauton spoke up. 'It's got a point, sir – how do we know they're who they say they are?'

'You said they were,' said Gaux.

'You can't blame me, sir. I'm only as good as my programmer, and that was you.'

Nick stepped forward. 'Of course we're who we say we are.'

'Prove it,' said Bly.

Nick looked at his teammates. 'Everyone turn around.'

They all turned around, once again displaying the names of the world's best footballers.

Bly looked at the names on the shirts and then at the team. 'Not good enough. I can't let you in.'

Gaux looked at Nauton. 'What can we do?'

'Leave this to me, I know how to handle

someone who works behind a counter,' said Phil, as he pushed his way to the front. He plonked his backpack on to the counter and unzipped the top. His hand disappeared inside, pushing past numerous packets of popping candy and crisps. 'I believe we have our documents here,' he said, as he handed a Curly Wurly over to Bly.

One of Bly's tentacles took the toffee-chocolate treat, unwrapped it and tossed it into its open mouth. Bly chewed for a moment, then a huge smile appeared on its tiny face. 'Those documents seem to be in order.'

'Ah, good,' said Gaux. 'So, we can pass through?'

'Wait,' said Bly. 'Does anyone have anything to declare?'

'I have nothing to declare but my genius,' said Eddie.

'Yep,' said Bly, 'heard that old one before as well.' Two tentacles reached over and grabbed Eddie, lifting him over the desk. 'I'll just take a quick look.'

The others could hear Eddie's screams as they

waited for their forms to be stamped.

Two minutes later and Eddie was deposited back over to their side of the desk, looking quite annoyed.

'You OK?' asked Nick.

'I CAN'T HEAR YOU!' shouted Eddie, as he waggled his fingers inside his ears. 'WHY WOULD IT LOOK FOR MY GENIUS INSIDE MY HEAD?'

'Beats me,' said Nick. 'There's nothing in there,' he chuckled.

'I CAN'T HEAR YOU!' shouted Eddie.

'Nauton will fix you,' said Gaux.

Nauton clomped over and slapped Eddie on the back, nearly flattening him. 'Can you hear now, sir?' said Nauton.

'DEFINITELY!' shouted Eddie, who looked close to collapsing. 'PLEASE, DON'T DO THAT AGAIN.'

'Hold out your hands,' said Bly. Everyone held out the palm of their hand and Bly quickly stamped each one. 'Enjoy your stay.'

Nick looked at his palm. Stamped there was the

word: *Bigpu*!

He giggled. 'I've got a Bigpu in my hand.'

Mia shook her head. 'I can't believe I'm with you weirdos on behalf of our entire species.'

'It was just a joke,' said Nick. 'You should try it one time, you might like it.'

'Stop talking to me,' said Mia.

They walked through customs and on the other side were met by a delegation from the GUFF. Their leader floated towards them on a hover chair. He was a hideous, silver-skinned, legless Quillian, with an enormous bald head. Sweat dripped from it and ran into one of his three chins.

'Who's this?' whispered Nick.

'It's Squirmo. Head of the GUFF,' whispered Gaux.

Squirmo stopped in front of the team. 'Welcome to Bigpu,' he said. His voice was all crackly. 'You must be this year's wildcard, yes?'

Gaux said they were.

'Good, good. Well, let's take a look at you.' He put his left hand to his temple and focused his eyes. Using his mind control, he forced Nick and the other teammates' arms up into the air and then spun them around 360 degrees. 'They look fit and healthy. I bet they make good strong workers.'

'What?' said a confused Nick.

'Do that to me again and I'll show you how strong we are,' said Mia.

'Feisty,' said Squirmo. 'You'll make worthy opponents. Now, you come from Earth, correct?' They all nodded. 'Tell me of your home world . . . Are there precious metals?'

*Why is he asking this?* thought Nick.

'The only thing you need to know is that we're gonna win this whole thing,' said Mia.

Squirmo tapped his temple. 'I'll keep that in mind.' He spun around and flew off.

Nauton shuffled them off and out of the spaceport. They flagged down a double-sized hover cab and all got in. The driver, Gaux explained in a whisper, was an Illiot, a tiny race of people from the outer rim of the galaxy. *His eyesight must be poor*, thought Nick, as the driver was wearing glasses almost as big as his lemon-coloured head. They hooked over his rabbit-like ears and made his eyes look ten times too big for his face.

'Where to?' asked the driver.

'The Grand Bigpuvian Hotel,' said Gaux.

The cabbie took off at high speed, leaving the spaceport behind and heading for the centre of Oloo. They pulled on to the highway but it was packed solid in a traffic marmalade (similar to a traffic jam, but tastier).

'I know a shortcut,' yelled the cabbie. He cut off down a slip road, narrowly missing several other hover cars. They flew by Bigpuvian homes and shops, all of which looked expensive, polished and new. Gigantic stretch-limo hover cars were everywhere, taking the Bigpuvians to destinations across their amazing, futuristic city.

'The Bigpuvians look very rich,' said Nick.

'That's Clause 47 for you,' said the driver. 'They don't call it the Galaxy *World* Cup for nothing.'

*What does that mean?* thought Nick. But, before Nick had a chance to ask more, a flustered Gaux quickly spoke up, 'OK, I know a lot of things are happening fast, but there's a few things we need to go over about the tournament. Obviously, it's five-a-side, but with slightly different rules to what you're used to.'

The cab swerved and everyone hit the opposite window. 'AT LEAST WE'RE GETTING TO SEE ALL THE SIGHTS!' shouted Eddie, his nose squashed against the glass. For Phil, this was even worse than giving away his last Curly Wurly. Nauton held a sick bag to his mouth, as streams of vomit flew out.

'How much more can be in there?' said Nauton.

Gaux continued, 'The matches last thirty minutes each way. Ten minutes' extra time if it's a draw, and if there's still no winner, then penalties.'

The cab hit a speed bump and flew up. Everyone bashed their heads before flopping back into their seats.

Gaux rubbed his head. 'Oh, that reminds me, there's no head height either. There are throw-ins, corner kicks, and you're allowed into the opponent's box. The playing area is larger than you're used to, but not as big as eleven-a-side.'

The cabbie slammed on his brakes. Everyone shot forward and smashed into Phil's sick bag, bursting it. Gallons of sick spewed out on to the floor of the cab.

'We're here,' said the cabbie.

Gaux looked at the meter. '*Five thousand, five hundred yelks!* You must have seen us coming!'

'I did,' said the cabbie. 'These Ultra-optic Lenses are the best in the galaxy. Oh, and it's fifty yelks extra for the mess, plus tip.'

The cab sped off, leaving them outside the main entrance to the Grand Bigpuvian Hotel. Nick looked up. The glass-and-gold building majestically stretched up to the sky, disappearing into the clouds. Flags of different nations fluttered above the shimmering gold letters of the hotel's name. Spotlights shone back and forth across the entrance, revealing plush bilbow trees in all their Bigpuvian glory.

'Wow,' said Nick.

'Yes,' replied Gaux. 'Ten thousand rooms, restaurants, gymnasiums and swimming pools.'

'Swimming *cool*'s more like it,' said Sanjay.

Mia smiled for the first time since leaving Earth. She craned her neck to peer upwards. 'Things are looking up.'

The teammates all smiled as they headed for the main entrance.

'Stop,' said Gaux, 'where are you all going?'

Nick pointed. 'The hotel.'

Nauton and Gaux looked at each other and then burst out laughing. 'You don't think that we're staying here?' howled Gaux.

'Where are we staying, then?' asked Phil.

Gaux pointed next door and everyone's faces fell.

# CHAPTER SEVEN

The Scrappy Hotel was in stark contrast to the Grand Bigpuvian one, thought Nick. It was a dump. The desk clerk was an old Bigpuvian and like all Bigpuvians he was stocky, with dark green scaly skin and a long allidile face. He looked shocked to see so many people enter the hotel.

'You looking to lay low for a night or have you just got out of the slammer?' said Lonky, his name handwritten on a badge pinned to his dirty shirt.

'No,' said Gaux. 'We booked in advance.'

Lonky laughed, expecting a joke that did not

come. 'Wait, let me get this right – you made reservations, to stay *here*?'

'Yes.'

'For *more than one night*?'

'Yes.'

It was six minutes before Lonky stopped laughing. He checked the hotel computer and amazedly, confirmed their booking. He grabbed the keys and told them to follow him, leading them along a dingy hallway to a room at the back of the hotel.

'This is our deluxe suite: three doubles, a bunk bed . . . and it's en-suite, with an actual working toilet.' Lonky said the last part with a weird sense of pride. He unlocked the door and gestured for them to enter. Nick and Mia were first in and were greeted by a strange, six-foot-long hairy creature with big front teeth, lying on one of the double beds.

'Oh, sorry,' said Nick, 'wrong room.' They turned to leave.

'No, it's the right room,' said Lonky, 'that's just a rat. Go on, shoo!' Lonky waved his arms. The rat flopped off the bed and scurried out the window.

'That was a rat?' Mia shuddered.

'Yep,' said Lonky. 'You're lucky it wasn't a mouse; they're twice the size.' Mia rushed over and pulled down the window, only to reveal it had no glass.

'Yeah, I've been meaning to fix that,' said Lonky. 'Don't worry about it. As long as you stay awake, they don't bother you.'

Nick looked out of the empty window frame. The view was of the alleyway separating the hotels. Huge rats scurried away as the big double doors of the Grand Bigpuvian Hotel opened and the smell of delicious food wafted out.

'That's the service entrance for next door,' said Lonky, 'where they take in all the laundry and food supplies.'

'Do you serve food?' asked Phil, his belly empty from all the vomiting.

Lonky laughed for a full minute. 'You guys are a hoot!' He held out his hand and Gaux tipped him two yelks. This time, he didn't laugh. 'You want anything, steal it from next door.' With that, Lonky left.

Mia flopped on to a double bed. 'This one's mine. The rest of you will have to share.'

Nick quickly called the top bunk and Eddie crashed on to the bottom. Sanjay and Phil took one bed and Gaux and Nauton the other.

Mia stretched out. 'I'm so tired not even those rats will keep me up.'

'Me too,' said Nick, yawning. 'Hey Gaux, when's our first match?'

Gaux typed into his hand tablet. 'In seventeen minutes' time.'

'What?' everyone cried.

'We're exhausted!' said Mia.

'I need a nap,' said Nick.

'I'm starving,' said Phil.

'This is great!' said Sanjay.

'My ears have popped!' said Eddie. 'I can hear.'

'It's not my fault,' said Gaux. 'As soon as the GUFF discovered you were here, Squirmo quickly rescheduled your match. You weren't due to play till later this week, but the GUFF will do anything and everything to make sure the Bigpuvian team retain their title.'

Nick frowned. Why was it so important to the GUFF that the Bigpuvians didn't lose? 'There seems to be more going on than just a football tournament, Gaux. What aren't you telling us?' asked Nick.

'I'm telling you now. The Bigpuvians have won every single Galaxy World Cup since its inception: all nine trophies. They've never lost a match.'

'Nobody's that good,' said Nick.

'That's what everyone's been saying,' said Nauton.

'They must be cheating,' said Mia.

'*Exactly*,' said Gaux. 'We just don't know how they're doing it. On the pitch they always get the favourable decisions, and off it, the GUFF make sure they have the easiest path to the final.'

'They're fixing it,' said Nick.

'Precisely,' said Gaux. 'But nobody can prove it. Only this time, we have a secret weapon.'

'A *Death Star*?' asked Eddie.

'What? No,' said Gaux. 'The resistance came up with a plan.'

'There's a resistance?' asked Mia.

'Of course! We can't let them get away with it – the stakes are too high.'

Nobody had a chance to wonder what those stakes might be, as Gaux continued with his speech. 'Their plan was to find a team so good it wouldn't matter what the Bigpuvians threw at them, they'd win it anyway. The resistance have been scouring the galaxy for the past two years for a team capable of beating them.'

'Sounds good. I hope you find them,' said Eddie.

'It's us, dummy,' said Mia.

'Correct,' said Gaux. 'The resistance risked their lives by fixing it for your planet to be this tournament's wildcard entry. Don't you see? *You* are the ones who are going to break the Bigpuvians' stranglehold on the tournament. *You* are the ones who are going to change everything. The fate of the galaxy rests in your capable feet. What do you say to that?'

'This is by far the weirdest detention I've ever done,' said Phil.

Nick giggled. '*Ha*, by detention, he meant pre-match warm-up. Didn't you, Mbappé?'

'Yes! Mbappé! That's me, Ronaldo,' said Phil, smiling.

'I still don't understand,' said Mia. 'Why would the resistance risk their lives? Who cares if they win every tournament? What difference does it make?'

'All the difference,' said Gaux. 'If we let them get away with that, who knows what else they'll do?'

'Sir,' said Nauton, 'it's come to my attention that we have five players but no goalkeeper.'

Gaux looked alarmed.

'Don't worry,' said Phil, 'I'm going in goal. Haven't you heard? Mbappé saves.'

'It's his Mothra,' added Eddie.

'Good,' said Gaux. 'We leave for the match in two minutes.'

Mia pulled Nick to one side and whispered, 'What did Gaux mean by *fate of the galaxy*?'

Nick shrugged. 'Maybe he was just being dramatic.'

Mia wasn't convinced. 'I think there's something else he isn't telling us.'

'I don't know,' whispered Nick, 'but there's

definitely something we're not telling him, and as soon as the first match kicks off, it'll be our fates resting in our pathetic feet.'

# CHAPTER EIGHT

The Eco-Emerald Stadium was a wonderful and weird sight.

Wonderful, because it appeared to have been grown from the green earth.

And weird, because of all the fans. As the team's taxi pulled up, they were mobbed. The fans surrounded the cab, rocking it from side to side, chanting, 'Wildcard! Wildcard!'

'The stadium is the greenest in the galaxy. Run entirely on solar and wind power,' said Gaux, appearing unfazed by the rabid fans.

'Cool. So how come we've got fans?' said a

bewildered Nick.

'Many neutral planets choose to support the wildcard entry,' said Gaux.

They squeezed out of the taxi and pushed through the chanting fans. Inside the stadium they were directed straight to their changing room. It seemed no different from the ones on Earth: benches to sit on, a changing zone for each player, showers and a tactic board. In the centre of the room stood a treatment table, covered in a big white sheet (something lay hidden underneath).

'Those fans were unbelievable,' said Nick.

'Get used to it,' said Gaux, 'the further we go in the tournament, the crazier the fans become.'

'I felt like one of the Beatles,' said Eddie.

'Yeah, you're a cockroach,' laughed Mia.

Gaux leant over and whispered to Nauton, 'Why are they always so rude to one another?'

'According to my databanks, sir, it's locker-room banter. It helps to build team morale.'

'Really?' Gaux turned to face the team and said, 'You're all a bunch of stinking cockroaches.'

The team stared back at him.

'That was a bit harsh,' said Phil.

'Yeah, first you abduct us, then you drag us across the galaxy, dump us in the hotel from hell – and now you insult us,' said Nick.

Gaux turned to Nauton. 'What's going on? You said it would help.'

Nauton whispered in Gaux's ear, 'They might just need a hug, sir.'

Gaux turned back to the team, smiling, and with arms outstretched, approached Mia for a hug.

'Take one more step and you'll be back in orbit,' she said.

Gaux turned sharply to Nauton. 'We need to have a serious look at your programming.'

Before this got any more awkward, Eddie changed the subject. 'Do we have new strips? 'Cause these ones are smelly.'

'And mine's covered in sick,' said Phil.

Sanjay sneezed.

'Unfortunately, with the change in times, your new strips aren't ready yet. But they will be here for the next match.'

Eddie giggled and said under his breath, 'Too

bad we won't.'

'What was that, Messi?' asked Gaux.

'Erm . . . just, it's too bad we won't have them for this match.'

'Yes,' said Gaux, 'but we have provided new football boots.'

Gaux whipped off the sheet from the treatment table to reveal five pairs of brightly coloured boots. They looked huge – at least size thirty.

Nick picked up a pair. 'Fee, fi, fo, fum.'

'Ronaldo's right,' said Mia. 'These would be a perfect fit – if we were clowns.'

Gaux chuckled. 'Of course, Earth hasn't invented flexi-fabric yet. These are Bendy Boots. Try them on!'

Nick shrugged and stepped easily into the size thirty boots with his size seven feet. All his teammates' eyes widened as they watched the boots flex and shrink to mould themselves perfectly to fit Nick's feet.

'Wow!' he said. 'These are the most comfortable boots I've ever worn in my life.'

All the other teammates quickly grabbed a pair

and tried them on.

'Mine don't fit,' said Eddie.

'You've got them on your hands,' said Nick.

'Oh, right.'

Gaux glanced nervously towards Nick. 'Is Messi OK?'

Nick smirked. 'Of course. He's Argentinian – hand of God and all that. He'll be fine.'

'Do I have any flexi-gloves?' asked Phil.

'Ah, yes,' said Gaux. 'They're called Give 'n' Take Gloves.'

'Well, give them here – I'll take them.'

Gaux passed them over. They, too, looked big enough to fit King Kong. Phil put them on, and they shrank to fit his hands to perfection. The first thing he grabbed was his backpack, and he slung it on.

'You won't need that, Mbappé,' said Gaux.

Phil looked deadly serious. 'Where I go, it goes.'

'So,' said Nick, 'are you going to tell us how you want us to play?'

Gaux laughed. 'Do I really need to tell the Earth's best players how to play football?'

'Yes,' came the team's reply.

'*Really?*' Gaux looked anxiously towards Nauton.

Nick nervously laughed. 'Of course we know how to play, right guys?' His teammates all smiled and gave a thumbs up. 'We just need some tips on the opposition . . . Like, how to beat them?'

'Oh right,' said Gaux. 'Don't worry, Nauton has detailed files on all the teams. Nauton, how can the team defeat the Zzllontis?'

Cogs whirled and buttons flashed. 'Simple,' said Nauton. 'You score more goals than them.'

'Yeah, but how do we score more goals?' asked Nick.

Gaux looked at Nauton for the answer. More cogs whirled. 'When you have the ball, pass to your own players, then shoot.'

'What is the Zzllontis team like?' asked Mia.

After three minutes, Nauton had his answer. 'They're rubbish.'

'See?' said Gaux. 'You've nothing to worry about.'

An official entered the changing room and told

them it was time.

Nick looked at his team. 'The Galaxy World Cup . . . if only Mr Barton and Mrs Hawn could see us now.'

'Oh, they will,' said Gaux.

'What? How?' asked Nick.

'When we first entered Earth's orbit, Nauton set up a satellite relay station. Images will be beamed back to every nation in every language. The whole planet will be watching.'

# CHAPTER NINE

Back on Earth, all the teammates' parents and guardians had gathered together in the school gym, along with concerned classmates, teachers, Ernie's United and the police. The team's unexplained disappearance was now into its twenty-third hour.

Nick's parents were only here tonight, together, for the sake of their son. Both blamed each other for Nick's sudden disappearance (as well as everything else).

'This is all your fault,' said Mrs Wilson.

'My fault? If he was living under my roof, he

wouldn't have gone missing!' screamed Mr Wilson.

Eddie's grandma sat in her wheelchair, quietly knitting at the side of the hall as others barked and argued around her. She was all alone, as Eddie's mother was a free-spirit activist, who was off around the world, trying to save it. Eddie had never known his father – he was convinced it was Darth Vader.

The Singh family looked lost. They stood holding a photo of their darling young boy. Sanjay's and the other kids' disappearances did not compute!

Mia's parents and five older brothers were there. 'If she doesn't come back, we should sue the school,' said one of her brothers.

The Beattys, including Phil's younger brother and sister, had closed their shop to be there. Mrs Beatty was distraught, tears flowing down her cheeks. Mr Beatty searched for a hanky, then looked back up to see his wife grabbing hold of a policeman. 'What are you doing in here?' she yelled. 'You should be out looking. My little Phil has been missing nearly a whole day! He'll be starving!'

The police were trying their best to calm everyone down, so they could discuss their options, when the TV screen behind them blinked on and two weird-looking aliens appeared. Everyone's phones beeped and the same two aliens appeared on their phone screens as well. Simultaneously, they popped up on every screen, from phones to laptops, across the globe. Everyone, from the President of the USA to King Charles, was now looking at the same two aliens.

'What's going on?' asked Mrs Hawn.

The alien on the left spoke first: 'Greetings, Earthlings! My name's Pog. Welcome to your first Galaxy World Cup competition!'

His co-presenter spoke next: 'And I'm Lug, and we'll be commentating on all thirty-one action-packed matches across the next two weeks, here on Planet Bigpu, on the other side of the galaxy.'

The aliens were strange to look at. They were thin, purple, blonde-wig-wearing creatures, with faces lifted more times than the FA Cup.

'Is this a joke?' asked Mr Barton.

'Now, I know you'll probably think this is a joke,' said Pog, 'but you've been selected as this year's wildcard into the competition.'

'And here are the team representing you at the tournament,' said Lug. 'Cristiano Ronaldo, Lionel Messi, Alex Morgan, Erling Haaland and Kylian Mbappé, collectively known as . . . Earth United!'

In the school gym everyone's jaws dropped open, whilst Eddie's grandma dropped a stitch for the first time ever, as up on the TV screen appeared . . . Nick, Mia, Eddie, Sanjay and Phil.

'*Earth United?*' said Lucas. 'Earth's Idiots is more like it. Mr Barton said six laps around the park, not the Milky Way.'

Mrs Singh looked distraught. 'When I said I wanted Sanjay to get out more, I wasn't thinking the other side of the galaxy.'

'Who's going to work the Saturday shift at the shop now?' asked Mr Beatty.

The Earth United players' faces were beamed all over the planet. The entire Earth's population now knew what Gaux did not: these were definitely not the world's best players. The real world's best players – Ronaldo, Messi, Morgan, Haaland and Mbappé – couldn't believe their eyes. They immediately rang their agents, asking for more money.

Mrs Beatty grabbed hold of Mrs Hawn. 'What are you waiting for? Launch the rockets! Get after them!'

'The school doesn't have any rockets, Mrs Beatty,' said Mrs Hawn.

'Call the prime minister, then,' said Mrs Wilson.

'I'm pretty sure Britain doesn't have any space rockets either,' said Mrs Hawn.

'We have to do something,' added Mrs Singh.

All the other parents agreed and turned on the chief inspector. 'Do something!' they screamed.

'There's nothing I can do,' he said. 'There's nothing anyone can do. They're stuck there.'

Pog and Lug went on to explain the competition and what was at stake, finishing with Clause 47.

The colour drained from Mrs Hawn's face. 'Did they just say what I think they said?'

Even the unflappable Lucas Marshall looked shaken. 'Yeah,' he said. 'If the Earth Idiots don't win, we're finished.'

# CHAPTER TEN

Earth United's players lined up in the tunnel, waiting to enter the arena. Nick had never been this nervous in his entire life. He couldn't believe he had been made the captain – he didn't know anything about leading a team. However, he didn't want to let down his teammates. It was time to face his fears. He pushed down his nerves, gritted his teeth and stood tall.

'Are you trying to hold a fart in?' asked Eddie.

'What? *No*.'

'What's with the funny face then?'

'I'm just psyching myself up for the match.'

The Zzllontis players came out of their changing room and stood side by side with Nick and the others. Nick checked out the player on his left. His yellow body was thick and heavyset. He had a large, round head with an enormous nose – Nick's entire face could have easily fit into any one of his three nostrils.

Nick turned his head and whispered to Mia, 'You could easily sink your teeth into one of those noses.'

'I'd rather not,' she whispered back.

Phil was the last Earth player in line behind Sanjay. Someone tapped his shoulder and he turned to see a smiling Bigpuvian, wearing a headset. She whispered something to him. He thought for a moment, before whispering back his reply. The Bigpuvian smiled and dashed off. Music blared and both teams were directed out of the tunnel and into a suns-filled (there were two in the sky) arena.

'Wow,' said an awestruck Nick. Every seat in the 200,000-capacity stadium was filled. Most of which by the Zzllontis' fans. They were very noisy, singing out the Zzllontis' football chant: 'Zzllontis! Zzllontis! We get the ball, we never miss.'

The stadium's tannoy system drowned them out as it announced for all inside to stand for the planetary anthems.

'Do we even have one?' asked Mia.

'Well,' said Phil, 'when we were in the tunnel a Bigpuvian approached me and asked us for our anthem.'

'And what did you say?' said Nick.

'Please say it was the "Imperial March" from *Star Wars*, by John Williams?' said Eddie.

Phil's reply was drowned out by the playing of the Zzllontis' planetary anthem. The Zzllontis players stood up tall and proud, with both arms aloft (the Zzllontis' salute). It was a big, bold, brassy tune that built up momentum as it went along, climaxing with a triumphant drum-based finish. The Zzllontis' fans screamed for their team and then fell silent, as they awaited the Earth's anthem.

Nick stood up straight and tall awaiting Mozart, or Beethoven. To his horror he recognized the song from the opening beat. This was no Mozart or John Williams, even. This was 'Shake It Off' by Taylor Swift. Nick looked at Phil.

'What have you done?' He turned to Mia, expecting her to be just as angry. However, Mia was now dancing along to the chorus.

'What?' she said. 'I like it.'

The song finished and the teams began to shake the Zzllontis' pincer claws, as they did not have any hands. Sanjay moved down the line of players, sneezing, as he greeted them.

The Robotic Ref rolled on to the pitch, holding the ball. Their gunmetal-grey, cylindrical body (with camera attached) sat on top of a large silver ball, allowing them to roll in any direction. The Ref called Nick over, along with the Zzllontis' captain. The Zzllontis player shook Nick's hand and passed over a Zzllontis pennant.

Nick had nothing to give in return. 'One moment.' He dashed off towards Phil in goal (and his backpack), returning a moment later to hand over a packet of salt and vinegar crisps. The Zzllontis captain's nostrils flared in bewilderment.

The Ref, with his stick-like arms, flicked up a strange green coin, pointed at Nick and in an electronic voice said, 'Heads or feet?'

'Feet,' replied Nick.

The coin landed on the grass.

'Feet it is,' said the Ref. 'You get to pick who kicks off.'

'We'll kick off.'

The Ref sped off and dropped the ball on the centre circle. A countdown began around the stadium, with all the fans chanting, 'Five . . . four . . . three . . . two . . . one!'

The Ref blew his whistle and Nick kicked off. The ball landed at Eddie's feet. He turned and ducked to the right, then jinked to the left before unleashing a ferocious shot towards the . . .

'Goallll!' screamed Eddie, as he slid on his knees in celebration. But his teammates did not join in.

'Well,' said Gaux from the sideline, 'that's the most amazing own goal I've ever seen. The Zzllontis are one–nil up.'

Phil grabbed the ball out of his net and kicked it back to Nick, who was still on the centre spot.

'We're shooting that way, Ed— I mean, Messi,' pointed Nick.

Eddie laughed, embarrassed. Nick restarted the game and this time passed to Mia. The Zzllontis' midfielder easily took the ball off her and passed to a teammate. He in turn passed to another Zzllontis player. Earth United tried, but couldn't get close to the ball.

'What's going on, Nauton?' said Gaux. 'They're rubbish! They look like headless floottells.'

'I believe on their planet floottells are called chickens, sir.'

On the pitch, Mia threw herself in front of the ball, just as the Zzllontis striker was about to shoot. However, before they actually kicked the ball, the Zzllontis striker sneezed. The single biggest sneeze in recorded galactic history. Snot globs the size of basketballs flew out of their gigantic nostrils and covered Mia from head to foot.

The whole stadium rocked with laughter.

''Snot funny!' screamed Mia.

Nick pointed. 'Look!' The rest of the Zzllontis team had joined the striker and were sneezing and sneezing and sneezing! They couldn't stop. Fans and officials were diving for cover as giant globs of Zzllontis snot flew from the players' noses.

'I think they've caught my sniffles,' said Sanjay. 'And I thought I was only good at computer viruses.'

The Ref blew for the Zzllontis' team doctor to come on to the pitch, but as soon as he did, he too caught the cold and began to sneeze. Then a single Zzllontis fan started to sneeze, before a Mexican wave of sneezing broke out around the stadium.

'They weren't kidding . . . This *is* the greenest stadium in the galaxy,' said Nick, laughing.

The Robotic Ref rolled through the sea of snot and consulted with the now-sneezing Zzllontis coach. A moment later, and the Ref crossed both arms and blew the whistle three times.

Gaux splashed through the snot, running to the team, his face colour changing from green to pink with happiness. 'The Zzllontis players can't continue – they've forfeited the match.'

'We *won*?' said a shocked Mia and Phil.

Sanjay sneezed in triumph.

'Bless you, Haaland,' said Nick.

'Who got player of the match?' asked Eddie. 'I mean, I did score, after all.'

Nick wrapped an arm around Sanjay. 'Sorry Messi, but hands down it's Haaland's cold who gets it.'

The Earth United players waded off the pitch, victorious, to a chorus of boos and sneezes from the Zzllontis crowd.

In the tunnel, the Zzllontis players were gracious in defeat and shook hands with the winning team. Both sets of players were about to swap shirts but declined, as they were either covered in snot, sick, sweat or more snot.

Waiting for them in the changing room were two very serious-looking GUFF officials. One held a clipboard, the other a tray with small plastic tubs on it. On each tub was the surname of an Earth United player.

'I'm not impressed with the player of the match awards,' said Eddie.

'No,' said Gaux, 'those are for your urine samples. Each player must give one after every game, to prove there's no cheating.'

'A drug test?' asked Nick.

'It's compulsory,' said Gaux. 'The list of banned substances is very long: grontol X, ovaluk 237, rhubarb and custard, the list goes on and on.'

Mia whispered to her teammates, 'Don't let them test our shirts – god knows what substances they'd find.'

Back at the smelly gym, the screens changed from images of the game back to Pog and Lug.

'Earth United are victorious, but I still don't know how,' said Pog.

'I think it was their snot-to-shot ratio,' said Lug. 'Earth United turned out to be their bogey team.'

'What an achievement!' said Mr Singh, punching the air in triumph.

Everyone joined in the celebration – everyone except Lucas and Mr Barton.

'We got lucky that time,' said Mr Barton.

'I know,' said Lucas. 'These fools are celebrating. Don't they realize the fate of the Earth is in the hands of the worst team ever?'

# CHAPTER ELEVEN

The next morning, the team found themselves sneaking into the alley that separated the two hotels. Like one of the giant rats, they all crouched down behind one of the enormous rubbish bins.

'Remind me why we can't just take the front door again?' asked Mia.

'Because we're part of the resistance,' whispered Gaux.

None of them thought that made any sense. Fortunately, it was not long before a delivery hover van came down the alley. It parked in front of the service doors of the Grand Bigpuvian Hotel and beeped. The doors opened and a crew of Illiots filed out of the hotel. They opened the back of the van and began unloading boxes.

'That's our cue,' said Gaux. The whole team pushed into the line with the Illiots, collected a box each and marched into the hotel.

Inside, the kitchens were hustling and bustling. Illiot cooks were frying up delights from across the Milky Way, while Illiot waiters were in and out, shuttling meals to the hotel's restaurants. The team dropped their boxes at the larder, then each grabbed a plate of food and followed a waiter out of the kitchen.

They slipped along a hallway and saw an irate Illiot maître d' heading their way. They dropped their plates and followed Gaux as he turned sharply to the left and into the laundry room. The noise inside was deafening, as hundreds of washing machines and dryers spun round and round.

Sanjay spotted a laundry trolley and pulled out a football strip eight times bigger than his own. 'Look at this.'

'That's the Derlerb team's football strip. Their squad are staying here at the hotel,' said Gaux.

'Must be nice,' said Nick.

'How many of the other teams are?' asked Mia.

Gaux began counting on his fingers. 'Erm . . . all of them.'

'How come we aren't?' said Eddie.

Before Gaux could answer, an Illiot laundry crew entered, carrying fresh bundles of washing. The team dived for cover, hiding inside a laundry trolley full of freshly washed and spun strips. They smelt of lucidous roses (not yet available on Earth), hiding any trace that they were there. The trolley began to move. The Illiot worker couldn't believe how heavy the load was, as he struggled to push it out of the laundry room and into the ironing one.

Eventually, he hooked the trolley up to the ironing machine's pulley system and left the room. The laundry trolley was hoisted into the air, before being tipped upside down. Out fell the team and strips on to the steam press area.

'Quick! Everyone off!' Gaux commanded. They rolled off with surprising speed, just as the red-hot steam press came down, flattening the strips.

Nick wiped the sweat from his brow. 'That's one way to iron out the creases in our game.'

'Even your jokes are obvious.' Mia rolled her eyes.

The team followed Gaux out of the ironing room and along a carpeted hallway until they reached the hotel's lobby.

To the left of them, eight Bigpuvian workers staffed a check-in desk made of solid ourk (the tallest trees in the galaxy). A variety of strange-looking guests, from Wartles to Glompers, were coming and going. The place was a hive of activity. Illiot bellhops were pushing cases to and from the hotel. To their right was the hotel's entrance, and across the vast lobby (the size of ten Illiot football pitches) were the numerous lifts and one set of stairs.

'How are we going to make it across to the lifts without being seen?' said Phil.

'We're not going to the lifts. We need the stairs – nobody uses them,' said Nauton.

'Same difference,' replied Phil.

'We need a diversion,' said Nick.

The gods of the universe (Bhigg and Bhanng) were obviously looking down on them, as at that exact moment, the doors of the hotel opened and in walked the Bigpuvian football team and their head coach, Zaph. Last to enter, surrounded by adoring fans, was their star player. The banners in the spaceport did not do justice to the true awesomeness of Clawtic. His strong allidile body would have made the Hulk look puny, and his face seemed to be chiselled from the rocks of Goglebe (the hardest rocks in the Milky Way).

'It's the GOAT,' said Nick.

'Pelé's here?' Eddie scanned the lobby for his auntie's prize-winning goat.

'No, Messi, he means Clawtic,' said Gaux. 'I told you, he's the greatest player in the galaxy. He's scored more goals than anyone and he's never missed a penalty.'

'This is our chance! Let's go,' said Nick. They moved out and joined the mass of Clawtic's fans. Squashed and squeezed, they moved slowly across the lobby, as Clawtic signed autographs and paused for selfies. Somehow, Mia was thrust to the front and came face to face with Clawtic. At seven feet two, he towered over Mia.

He looked her up and down, and in a deep booming voice said, 'You're a strange little ugly one. Do you want an autograph?'

Mia wanted to punch his lights out, but Nick nudged her to remind her not to. She smiled and said, 'I don't have a pen or paper.'

Clawtic grabbed a pen from his pocket, took hold of Mia, and scrawled his name across her forehead. 'There,' he said. 'You look much better now.' He turned and marched on.

Mia was about to jump on his back, but was pulled away by her teammates. They moved on with the crowd, until they took their chance to slip away to reach the stairs.

'Horrible beast,' said Mia, as she rubbed Clawtic's signature off her head.

'You should have kept it,' said Eddie. 'Probably be worth something in the future.'

Mia grabbed Eddie's shirt sleeve and wiped the remains away. 'You have it.'

'Enough bickering – let's go,' said Gaux. He led

them up two flights of stairs, along another corridor and round a bend. 'Good teamwork. I knew we'd make it to the training room.'

A sign in front of them pointed left for the multi-gym and right for the football pitches. Following the right sign, they arrived at their destination. Nick peeked inside and gave a thumbs up. 'It's empty.'

The pitch was brand new, fitted out with the latest AstroTurf surface.

'How long do we have the pitch for?' asked Mia.

'Erm . . . till somebody comes,' said Gaux. 'We haven't actually booked it. Why did you think we just did all that sneaking in? So, let's get on with it. Nauton has devised a warm-up and exercise plan.'

Nauton instructed everyone to line up and they began with simple stretches and jogging on the spot.

'Warm-up complete,' said Nauton. 'Now, on the ground and give me twenty sit-ups.'

Phil raised his hand. 'I can't do sit-ups. Sit-downs, on the other hand, I'm brilliant at.'

'What about press-ups?' asked Nauton. Everyone raised their hand.

'Everything that's up, I'm not down with,' said Phil.

'Mbappé's right,' said Nick. 'Let's just get on with the footy training.'

Nauton looked at Gaux, who shrugged, as if to say, *whatever*.

They started with running and dribbling. Nauton set up cones three feet apart and instructed the team to dribble in and out, the length of the pitch, before passing the ball back and sprinting to the start. Sanjay went first, followed by Eddie, Mia then Phil.

Nick was just about to take his turn, when Gaux shouted, 'Run!'

'I just did my running,' said Phil.

'No, somebody's coming!' yelled Gaux. They dashed for the fire exit.

Back at the hotel, Lonky was waiting to greet them. 'You've had a delivery. I put it in your room.' He held out his hand and waited for a tip that never came.

In their room was a big brown box. Nauton ripped it open to find some basic everyday clothes and their new football kits.

'Super cool,' said Sanjay.

The top was green with a football planet on the front. The shorts were sky blue, and there were white socks. Mia pushed everyone out of the way and searched through the box. She let out a sigh of relief as she found the only long-sleeved top. 'It's to cover my tattoo,' she said.

'And don't worry,' said Gaux, 'we'll have everyone's names printed on the backs in time for tomorrow's match.'

'We're playing tomorrow?' asked an exhausted Nick.

'This is the Galaxy World Cup,' said Gaux. 'The games come thick and fast.'

'So are you actually gonna tell us how you want us to play?' asked Mia.

'Yeah, what formation?' added Nick.

'That's easy,' said Eddie. 'Four-four-two.'

'There's only five of us, Messi,' replied Nick.

'We don't even know who we're playing,' said Sanjay.

Nauton beeped. 'Our next round opponents are

the Bzard Blasters.'

'Are they called that because they shoot hard?' asked a worried Phil.

'No,' said Nauton. Phil breathed a sigh of relief. 'They just blast into the opposition. They put three of their last opponents into the hospital.'

'*Hospital?*' said the entire team.

# CHAPTER TWELVE

Their next match was at a different stadium, the brand-new Quark Arena. It had been specially built for the tournament and gleamed in the light of the moons (four, of varying sizes, hung in the night sky). Earth United's cab arrived for their late kick-off, just as their opponents' team bus pulled up. The Bzard team stepped out to cheers from their fans. They were stocky little blue things, no bigger than five feet, with small pointy heads and six green eyes.

'Woah . . .' said Sanjay. 'Look at them.'

Each Bzard player had eight arms, and every

arm bulged with muscle.

Gaux could see the fear in his team's eyes. 'Don't worry, you don't play football with your arms.'

'I do,' said Phil.

'You play it with your brain,' continued Gaux.

'We've no chance, then,' said Nick.

'Speak for yourself,' said Mia.

Gaux and Nauton shuffled the team into the stadium.

Twenty minutes later, the planetary anthems had been played and the players were walking down the line, shaking hands. This took about ten minutes, as Earth United had to shake each of the eight hands of the opposition.

The two captains met in the middle and exchanged pennants (a tube of Smarties, in Earth's case). The Bzard captain won the toss and elected to kick off. The Bzard Blasters ran off to their side of the pitch. Earth United huddled together on their side.

'OK,' said Nick, 'let's try and keep the score down till half-time. Who knows, maybe we'll still be in it and can nick a goal in the second half? And remember, stay out of their way.'

They all bumped fists and broke for the match. The Ref blew the whistle, and the game began.

Back on Earth, the whole planet cringed and screamed at their screens as the Bzards easily blasted through the Earth's defence. Mia, Nick and the others were simply brushed aside as the Bzards shoulder-barged them out of the way and passed to their striker. He collected the ball and banged a shot into the bottom left-hand corner, giving Phil no chance to save it.

'One–nil to the Bzard Blasters,' said Pog.

'If they keep playing like this, Earth United are in for a long, hard night,' added Lug.

A second Bzard goal was quickly followed by a third, as Earth United were knocked back and forth across the pitch.

'They're too strong,' said Mia, rubbing her bruised and battered shoulders.

'We'll have to be stronger, then,' said Nick.

'Remember, Gaux thinks we're the Earth's best. It's our lives on the line.'

'I can't watch any more of this,' said Gaux, his face turning dark blue. 'We're being destroyed.' He covered his eyes with his hands.

'I don't blame you, sir,' said Nauton. 'If these are Earth's best players, I wouldn't like to see the worst.'

Nick kicked off and passed the ball to Mia, who launched it towards the first approaching Bzard player. It smacked off their lower right arm.

The Ref blew the whistle. 'Hand ball!'

Earth United pushed their players up the pitch and Nick took the free kick. Once again, he tried to pass, but the ball struck the Bzard defender's arms. The Ref blew again for a hand ball and another free kick.

'Their stupid arms keep getting in the way of our passing,' said Eddie.

'Who cares?' said Nick. 'It's getting us up the pitch.'

The Earth United players were now deep into the Bzards' half for the first time in the game. Nick once again took the free kick. He passed it to Mia, who dodged past one Bzard player.

'Pass, pass!' screamed Eddie.

But Mia wasn't passing. She was a one-woman team. She shot the ball towards the Bzard defender who was inside the box. It hit off all four arms on the left side of their body.

The Ref blew his whistle and pointed to the spot. 'Penalty!'

Nick scooped up the ball. 'Here, you take it – you're our best player.'

'I was taking it anyway,' she said, snatching the ball from him.

Mia placed the ball on the penalty spot. She composed herself, took a deep breath, counted to three, ran towards the ball and smashed it in to make it three–one!

The Ref blew the whistle and the match restarted. Eddie charged towards the Bzard player, slid in and took the ball. He tried to pass upfield, but the ball (again) hit off the player's outstretched arms.

Sanjay took the free kick. He got another free kick straight away, twenty yards up the pitch, as the ball clattered off two Bzard players' arms. It was three yards outside the Bzard box, a perfect spot for a shot at goal. Mia placed the ball and lined it up. She looked at the Bzards' defence, who had now formed a wall in front of their keeper. Nick thought, *Just be like Morgan*. Mia ran, kicked the ball and bent it around the wall, past the keeper and into the back of the net. She squealed with joy and ran off to celebrate.

'What a goal, sir!' said Nauton, who began to celebrate by doing the Peter Crouch.*

Gaux, who was still covering his eyes, said, 'What's that, five–nil?'

'No sir, three–two, we're right back in it.'

Now looking through his three fingers, Gaux checked the scoreboard. 'How?'

'I think the training's paid off, sir.'

Gaux smiled, and his face returned to its natural green colour. 'Come on, Earth United!'

United came on the attack again, moving up the pitch with free kick after free kick, eventually

---

* The Peter Crouch celebration is the opposite of the robot one and is the tallest celebration in the galaxy.

ending with another penalty. The Bzard team were furious.

'It's not our fault,' said Nick. 'Your arms are everywhere!'

'Morgan's on a hat trick,' said Lug. 'Can she do it?'

'She runs up and . . . goal!' screamed Pog. 'That's three all!'

Lug smiled. 'You've got to, well, *hand* it to them, I suppose – Earth United are back level.'

The Bzard team restarted the match and were on the attack when the Ref blew for half-time.

Back on Earth, and the old smelly school gym had become ground zero for Earth United supporters. People were flocking from all over the country. News crews were beaming constant images from inside around the globe. The parents and guardians of Earth United had basically moved in. They'd come together to form a group called Earth Re-United, with the aim of getting their children home.

Mia's five brothers were manning the door, charging an entrance fee, in order to buy ~~Xboxes~~ a rocket to bring their sister home. The Singhs were cooking up a pot of their favourite tikka masala, keeping everyone well fed. The Beattys had set up multiple giant screens, so everyone had a great view of the match. Eddie's grandma was knitting team scarves for the parents and fans. Mr and Mrs Wilson came out of the gym's changing rooms to discover they were both dressed in huge globe-like outfits. They looked like Mother and Father Earth.

'I was thinking I could be the team mascot,' said Mrs Wilson.

'Me too,' said Mr Wilson.

'We always did have the same ideas,' Mrs Wilson chuckled.

They both pulled out a song sheet. 'No way,' they both said. They stood side by side and began to sing:

*'United we stand,*
*United we fall,*
*United haven't got a clue about football.*
*Earth United!*
*Earth United!*

*United can't pass,*
*United can't score,*
*Even with a thousand shots*
*they'd miss a barn door.*
*Earth United!*
*Earth United!'*

Lucas and the other members of Ernie's United burnt with envy. 'It should be us at that tournament,' said Lucas. 'We beat those losers twenty-two–nil.'

Fans across the globe from China to Timbuktu were getting behind the team.

Even the US President cheered them on, despite not knowing one thing about soccer.[*] However, having watched the first half he was alarmed by how easily you could get over the wall. He would have to have his team investigate.

After a half-time team talk (of screaming) by the Bzards' coach, and utter disbelief by Earth United's, both teams ran back on to the pitch. The

---
[*] The GUFF does not recognize the word 'soccer'.

Earth players stopped dead and looked at the Bzard players in amazement.

'Where are their arms?' said Nick.

The Bzard Blasters marched back down to their side of the pitch, but none of their eight arms could now be seen. The Bzards' coach stood on the sideline with a huge grin on his face. He had instructed all his players (except the keeper) to tuck their eight arms inside their shirts. There would be no hand balls in this half of football.

'What now?' said Mia.

'Ronaldo?' said Phil, Sanjay and Eddie.

They were all looking to Nick, their captain. He gulped and shook his head. 'I have no idea,' he said. The panic started to rise – Gaux should never have made him the captain.

The whistle blew, Nick kicked off and the second half began. He passed to Eddie, who flicked it to Sanjay. Sanjay was tackled by a Bzard player, who then sent the ball up to a teammate. She tried to spin and shoot for goal. However, with her arms tucked inside her shirt she struggled for balance and clattered into Mia, sending her sprawling. The

Ref blew for a free kick.

Nick's eyes lit up. 'They've got no balance.'

'Neither do we,' said Eddie. 'We seem to play all down the right side.'

'No, I mean the Bzard players can't keep their balance with their arms tucked in.'

Nick took the free kick and passed to Eddie. Charging up the pitch, they easily passed back and forth to one another. The reason for this was, as the Bzard players tried to turn to get the ball, they lost balance and kept falling over. Eddie slid the ball perfectly to Nick, who missed a sitter and blazed over the bar. He slumped to his knees and held his head in his hands.

'This is why I don't pass,' said Mia.

From the sideline, Gaux tried to raise Nick's spirits. 'Don't worry,' he said, 'you'll get the next one.' Gaux's words lifted Nick. He got to his feet, determined to score the next goal.

For the next twenty-eight minutes, Earth United dominated the match. They were in the Bzards' half so often, Phil was getting bored. He fancied a packet of crisps (not yet available on Bigpu), but sadly realized he had used his last bag as the Earth's gift to the Zzllontis. However, he'd recently restocked his backpack with alien sweets, much to the annoyance of Gaux's wallet. He opened his backpack (which was tucked inside his goal area) and pulled out a packet of alien smelly jellies. Munching away, he watched as his teammates easily won possession back from the balance-less Blasters and launched wave after wave of attack.

The only two things keeping the Bzards in the match were their goalkeeper and Earth United's finishing. Apart from Mia, who was making the Bzard goalie save a string of fine shots, the other team members couldn't hit the floor if they fell over. Sanjay's shots seemed to break the laws of physics and fly off his boots at new invented angles. Eddie's kicks were so high over the bar they would land in row Quish (the last letter of the Bigpuvian alphabet). Nick did hit the post . . . sadly, it was with his face, as he dived to meet a cross and completely missed the ball.

With a minute to go, one of the Bzard players had had enough. He pushed his arms back out of his shirt and sprinted for the ball. Nick tried to pass to Mia and the ball smashed off the Bzard player's arms. The whistle blew, and Earth United had a free kick in a dangerous position.

The Bzard players lined up in a wall in front of their keeper (the player who had caused the free kick now had his arms back inside his shirt). Mia and Nick stood over the ball, waiting for the Ref to blow the whistle.

'What's your plan?' said Nick.

'Ten-pin bowling,' said Mia, smirking.

'What?'

But the whistle blew for her to take the free kick. She ran up to the ball and whacked it! This time, however, it did not fly over the wall. Instead, the ball smashed into the Bzard player on the far left. They wibble-wobbled, then fell over, crashing into the player next to them. This caused a domino effect, and the entire wall came crashing down, falling backwards, knocking the goalkeeper out of the way. The ball landed kindly at Sanjay's feet and he slotted home into an empty net.

'Strike!' screamed Mia.

All the Earth United players dived on to Sanjay to celebrate. On the sideline, Gaux and Nauton were cheering too. As soon as the Bzards restarted the match, the Ref blew for full-time. Earth United were into the quarter-finals.

# CHAPTER THIRTEEN

Back at the Scrappy Hotel and everyone was on Cloud Grump (nine in Bigpuvian). 'To celebrate our victory,' said Gaux, 'I have decided we shall go out tonight and enjoy a delicious meal.'

Everyone's bellies rumbled in agreement. Phil's backpack had fed them so far, but there was only so much chocolate they could eat!*

'Where's good then?' asked Mia.

'Well, we can't go into the city centre. After your

---

* Parents across the galaxy will find this hard to believe. Children can eat chocolate for three meals a day, seven days a week, for eternity.

victory today, you'll be mobbed by fans,' said Gaux.

'Well, we can't eat here,' said Nick. 'We'll die!'

'Where else is there?' asked Phil.

As if on cue, the service doors of the Grand Bigpuvian Hotel opened and the smell from its kitchens floated out and in through their window.

'Let's go!' hollered Nick, and the team followed him out of the open window.

'Wait,' said Gaux, looking inside his wallet. 'I was thinking somewhere cheaper . . .' But the team was already gone and heading towards the hotel. 'OK, but no starter or dessert.' Gaux looked at Nauton. 'You coming?'

'No point, sir. I'll stay behind and recharge my batteries.'

The Grand Bigpuvian Hotel had a total of fifty-seven restaurants, serving every type of food from across the Milky Way. There was seafood, deafood, vegetarian and vulcan. There were fast-food, slow-food and no-food restaurants. There was even a restaurant where the food could eat the diners – every taste was catered for.

There was no sneaking in, as this time the Earth United team marched through the front door as paying guests. Aliens murmured as they passed by, recognizing them from that evening's game.

They stood outside the lift and checked out all the restaurant names. 'There's so many,' said Sanjay.

'Which one should we pick?' asked a salivating Nick.

'Any,' said Phil. 'I'm starving.'

Gaux arrived and quickly checked the list, breathing a sigh of relief. 'Oh, thank goodness. They have a One, Two restaurant.'

The lift pinged, the doors opened, and everyone crammed in. Gaux pressed the button for floor 102.

'Floor 102? The view will be amazing,' said Sanjay.

Nick looked at Mia. 'What's a One, Two restaurant?'

She shook her head. 'Maybe it's football themed?'

The lift arrived, to reveal the One, Two restaurant was not football themed. In fact, it wasn't themed at all. It looked to Nick like a run-down soup kitchen, with long tables and bland white walls. On the far side of the restaurant was a wall of windows. Normally for Nick, windows were a good thing. This time, however, they were redundant. You couldn't see a thing through them.

'This restaurant is unfortunately located directly at cloud level. Due to this, and it being a One, Two restaurant, it cuts down significantly on the cost,' said Gaux, smiling.

An Illiot waiter shepherded the team to their table and placed menus in front of them.

Nick opened his menu and stared. 'Is that it?'

The menu only had two options: One or Two.

'That's the beauty of this place! They only serve two meals at any time,' said Gaux.

'But it doesn't even say what they are,' said Phil.

Gaux asked the waiter what the dishes of the day were.

'Number one is our homemade Flompa Wompa bars, best in town. And number two today is Truth Gloop Soup, guaranteed to bring spice to any dinner conversation.'

'I think I'll have a number two on Bigpu,'

laughed Eddie.

Everybody except Phil ordered the number two. 'I'll have the Flompa Wompa bars,' he said. 'Anything with a name like "gloop" can't be good for you.'

No sooner had their waiter taken away the menus, than she was back with their meals.

'That was quick,' said Mia.

'Yes,' said Gaux. 'Fast food is close to the speed of light on this side of the galaxy.'

Gloop Soup reminded the teammates of the school canteen's semolina pudding, the only difference being that this one looked edible.

'What is Truth Gloop Soup anyway?' asked Nick.

'To tell you the truth, I don't know,' said Gaux. 'But I do know that its taste makes you tell the truth.'

Mia ate a glob. 'It's gorgeous,' she said, 'and that's the truth.'

'How's the Flompa Wompa bars?' asked Eddie.

On Phil's plate were eight long, thin sticks of chocolate-covered fruit biscuit. He bit into one and a flavour unlike anything he'd tasted before filled his mouth.

'Oh, *Fox's Glacier Mints*,' he drooled. 'These put my beloved crisps to shame.'

'And they're so cheap!' added Gaux.

'Really?' Phil's eyes widened at the possibilities. 'I could make a small fortune.' He quickly summoned the waiter and ordered two hundred Flompa Wompa bars to go.

'Hey, Gaux,' said Nick, who was also now tucking into his soup, 'how many teams have you managed before us?'

'None,' laughed Gaux, with Truth Gloop dribbling down his chin. 'I'm making this up as I go along.'

Eddie was halfway through his bowl already. 'That's funny,' he said. 'Because we've never played for any teams before, either.'

Gaux chuckled, then his face froze. 'Huh? What do you mean?'

'We're not even footballers! We're not the real Messi or Ronaldo, we're just a bunch of kids!' said Eddie, as he told Gaux all their real names.

Gaux's face fell. 'Is this true?'

'Yes,' said Nick, Mia, Sanjay and Eddie, all of whom were now unable to lie.

Gaux dropped his spoon. 'It's all over! We'll never win the cup. I may as well drown myself now.' He fell face forward into what was left of Eddie's soup.

The Illiot waiter appeared tableside. 'Is everyone enjoying their meal?'

'Waiter, waiter!' said Eddie. 'I have an alien in my soup.'

'You should've gone with the number one,' said Phil. No sooner had he said this, than his face began to grow. His neck bulged, his cheeks swelled and his forehead expanded outwards. 'What is going on?' he yelled. His teammates watched, stunned, as his legs tripled in size and his hands inflated like giant balloons.

'He's expanding faster than the universe,' said Eddie.

'He must be allergic to whatever's in those bars,' said Nick.

'What do we do, Gaux?' asked Mia.

Gaux lifted his head from Eddie's bowl and Truth Gloop dripped down off his cheeks. It was clear by his face he'd never heard Mia's question, and he looked lost in his own defeated thoughts.

'Let's get Phil to Nauton,' suggested Sanjay. 'He'll know what to do.'

They dragged Balloon Phil back to the Scrappy Hotel. Nauton took one look at Phil and knew exactly what to do.

'Nothing,' he said.

'What?' came the team's collective reply.

'I've checked my databanks and it clearly states the only cure for Flompa Wompaness is time. He should be back to normal within the next four hours.'

'Four hours like this?' said Phil.

'Yes, I'm afraid so,' said Nauton. 'Now, what happened to him?' He pointed to Gaux, who was now lying flat out on the bed, staring lost towards the ceiling. 'Did the restaurant cost too much?'

Nick filled Nauton in on the night's events, explaining how they weren't actually the world's greatest footballers. 'We're just a bunch of kids.'

'Well, that explains . . . *everything*,' Nauton said.

'Can you fix Gaux?' asked Mia.

'He just needs a good night's rest,' said Nauton, and he brought his iron fist down on top of Gaux's head, knocking him out cold.

# CHAPTER FOURTEEN

Gaux awoke the next morning with an empty wallet, a splitting headache, and Nick, Nauton and the rest of the team (minus Sanjay) standing around his bed. He looked at Messi, Ronaldo and Morgan and it all came flooding back.

'Huh, here they are . . . *Earth United*. What a joke. You're only united in your lies and deceitfulness, nothing else! I should rename you *Earth Uninvited*.'

'Let us explain,' said Nick. 'We didn't tell you because we thought you'd vaporize us if you found out we weren't the real players.'

'Not if you'd told me straight away . . .' said Gaux.

'We didn't get a chance! You abducted us and dragged us to the other side of the galaxy before we even knew what was going on.'

'They have a point, sir,' said Nauton.

'Well, it's too late now,' said Gaux. 'This sorry lot aren't going to beat the Bigpuvians.'

'We've got this far,' said Mia.

'Blind luck.'

Nick sighed. 'Come on, Gaux, don't be like Lucas Marshall.'

'Who?'

'He says we're losers who'll end up working at the drive-through.'

'We're underdogs, of course,' said Phil. 'But our bite is worse than our bark.'

'Give us a chance,' said Eddie. 'I mean, you've never coached before.'

'Yes,' said Gaux, 'but I thought you'd *played* before.'

'We have,' said the team.

'Not against these players! How are you going to beat the team who's never lost a match?'

'One game at a time,' said Nick. 'Let's just concentrate on the next match first.'

'Sure,' said Gaux. 'It'll be your last.'

Sanjay came dashing out of the bathroom with a strange look on his face. 'Guys? The toilet's talking to me.'

'We know,' said Nick. 'It's what they do. It told me I need more fibre in my diet.'

'The toilet *talks*,' said a relieved Eddie. 'It wasn't a voice in my head!'

'Did it tell you that you seriously need to see a doctor as well?' asked Phil.

'No,' said Sanjay. 'I know the toilet talks. I have been to the toilet since we've been here. But this time it's different. Now, this might sound a bit potty, but the toilet wants to see us all and it's not happy.'

'Did somebody not flush?' asked Mia. Everybody looked at Eddie.

'It was one time!'

Two minutes later and everyone had squeezed

into the tiny en-suite bathroom. Lonky had mentioned that the toilet worked – and this was what he meant.

In a big thunderous voice, the toilet spoke. 'Gaux!' Orange and green lights lit up on either side of the cistern.

'Erm, yes?'

'Is everybody there, including the Earth United players?'

'Well that's debatable,' whispered Gaux.

'What was that?' asked the toilet.

'Yes, we're all here,' said Nick. 'Who's this?'

'I can't reveal my true name. You can call me Lou.'

'Who are you, Lou?' asked Phil.

'I am part of the resistance against the Bigpuvian Empire.'

'Why didn't you just come to our hotel room, like a normal person?' asked Mia.

'The resistance work in the shadows,' said Lou. 'Our identities must stay hidden.'

'OK, makes sense.'

'Gaux! Are you sure these are the correct players?'

Gaux looked at the team and they looked back

at him, pleading with their eyes for him to not spill the beans and reveal their true identities.

Gaux shook his head and said, 'They are Earth United.'

The team silently cheered in triumph.

'You're sure?' asked Lou. 'Because they don't look like the team we sent you to pick up. In fact, they look like a bunch of amateurs who've never kicked a ball in their lives.'

'Oh yeah?' said Nick. 'Then how come we're into the quarter-finals?'

'To tell you the truth, I have no idea,' replied Lou.

'We're just lulling everybody into a false sense of security,' said Mia.

*Brilliant*, thought Nick. 'Yeah, we're pretending to be rubbish, doing just enough to get through each round.'

'Well, you're making an exceptional job of it,' said Lou.

'Thank you,' said Phil.

'That wasn't a compliment,' said Lou.

'Thank you,' said Eddie.

'Something still doesn't smell right,' said Lou.

'Well, I definitely flushed,' said Sanjay.

There was a long minute of silence.

'Gaux, I hope for your sake they're who they say they are. There are rumours that the information we gathered on these players was corrupted somehow. And maybe their planet has not actually reached the required footballing level. That would mean the resistance has a mole . . . or maybe, a Gaux?'

'Never!' said Gaux. 'I'd never betray the resistance – you know that. You were the ones who fixed it for the Earth to be the wildcards.'

'Yes, but it was on your recommendation,' said Lou.

'Is that true, sir?' asked Nauton.

'Well, yes, I did put them forward. I mean, have you seen Ronaldo and Messi's stats? They're good enough to play for the Bigpuvians! But I didn't get the final pick on who was going to be the wildcard.'

There was another long minute of silence. 'I'll have to do some digging,' said Lou. 'Meanwhile, best of luck for the next match. You know how important this is, Gaux – the galaxy is depending on you.' And with that, Lou's lights faded and he was gone.

The team headed back into the bedroom.

'That was weird,' said Phil.

'I know,' said Nick. 'I can't believe we've just had a conversation with a toilet.'

'It's normal at my house,' said Mia, 'when my dad's had one too many down the pub.'

'What now?' asked Sanjay.

'What now?' echoed Gaux. 'Well, I've lied to the resistance and staked my life on Earth Uninvited winning this whole thing. If you don't, the resistance will . . .'

'Will what?' asked Mia. 'Flush us down the toilet?'

'What's left of us, maybe,' said Gaux.

Nick didn't like the sound of that. Just when they had got out from under the stress of Gaux discovering their true identities, they now had the resistance to deal with.

'What are they resisting, anyway?' asked Nick.

'I've already told you – the Bigpuvians' stranglehold on the tournament, that's what,' said Gaux.

'What have I done?' He flopped on to the bed and pulled a pillow over his head.

'Don't give up on us, Gaux,' said Nick. 'You picked Earth!'

'No, I put the Earth forward as a possibility – there's a difference,' said Gaux.

'But you believed in us,' said Mia.

'Yes . . . when I thought I was getting the Earth's best players.'

'We may not be the Earth United you thought you were getting, but we can do this,' said Nick. 'We've got a training session planned. Phil's got a talk prepared.'

'Let's hear it, then,' said Gaux, unconvinced.

Phil reached inside his backpack and pulled out a small tub of sweets. 'I have six different flavours, each guaranteed to give taste satisfaction.'

'Stop,' said Nick. 'What are you doing?'

'What you said.' Phil held up the sweets and rattled them. 'Do a talk on Tic Tacs.'

'*Tactics!*' screamed Nick. 'I said, do a talk on tactics!'

'Oh,' said Phil. 'That makes much more sense. I

don't know anything about tactics.'

'It's hopeless,' said Gaux. 'Do any of you know any tactics?'

Eddie raised his hand.

'Yes, Messi – erm, Eddie, I mean,' said Gaux.

'Is anybody else really frightened about going to the toilet now?'

'What are you talking about?' asked Gaux. 'Does anyone have a clue how to win the next match?'

'Score more goals than them, sir,' said Nauton.

'I give up,' said Gaux, flinging his hands in the air.

'We don't even know who we're playing,' said Mia.

'The Skyorls. Show them, Nauton,' said Gaux.

Nauton's breastplate flopped down to reveal a monitor. On it appeared five extremely thin aliens with eyes attached to antennae on either side of their orange heads.

'*Orange,*' said Mia. 'That's the tactic we use. We'll play Total Football like the great Dutch team of the 1970s.'

'You know we can't play, right?' said Nick.

'That's what I've been saying,' said Gaux.

'I'll just teach you the basics, then,' said Mia. 'And a few tricks, like the Cruyff turn.'

'What's that?' asked Phil.

'I think it's on the Dutch driving test,' said Eddie.

'OK, sounds like a plan,' said Nick. 'Are you in, Gaux?'

Gaux looked at the team. They looked back at him with puppy underdog eyes.

'We've got nothing to lose, sir,' said Nauton.

'Fine,' Gaux said. 'What else am I going to do? I'll coach you, but don't blame me when this all goes wrong.'

Everyone cheered. The team headed off to sneak back into the Grand Bigpuvian Hotel for training, and for the next two hours worked hard on their Dutch driving test.

# CHAPTER FIFTEEN

The Eco-Emerald Stadium was bouncing – literally – as the Skyorl fans jumped up and down to welcome their team on to the pitch. The Earth United fans were growing by the game and now filled an impressive twenty thousand seats of the arena. The fans weren't the only ones bouncing as the teams took to the pitch – Nick and the others bounced up and down as they walked.

'What's going on with the pitch?' asked Nick. It was made from a spongey yellow AstroTurf.

'The Skyorls have home advantage,' said Gaux. 'The turf resembles their home planet of Whey.'

'And you're only telling us this *now*?' growled an angry Mia.

Nick noticed the fans were holding up signs that read: 'Go Ronaldo!' 'Magic Morgan' and 'Ban Clause 47'. *What's Clause 47?* he thought.

With the planetary anthems over, Phil bounced his way down to his goal. His face turned green. 'This surface is not going to agree with me.'

The Skyorl team kicked off and went straight on the attack, skipping past Mia and Nick. Sanjay and Eddie bounced across the pitch from opposite sides, to cover. The Skyorl player bounced through between them, and Sanjay and Eddie clashed together, bashing heads. The player passed to the Skyorl skipper, who kicked for goal. Phil bounced off the springy surface and flew across the goalmouth with his arms outstretched. His fingertips connected with the ball, sending it wide. Landing on the nice soft springy surface, he said, 'I've changed my mind, I like this.' He then turned and vomited into his net.

'What a sick save!'

'You're right there, Pog,' said Lug. 'I think the

Whey planet playing surface seems to agree with the Earth's goalkeeper.'

The Skyorl player took the corner kick, floating it into the box, but Phil bounced up and easily collected the ball above everyone's heads. He threw the ball towards Nick, who took it down with his chest and then rolled it to Sanjay.

'Why are there two balls?' asked Sanjay.

Sanjay was still recovering from his head clash with Eddie – he must be seeing double, thought Nick. Sanjay had a fifty–fifty chance of kicking the right one. He failed. He swung his boot for the ball that was not there and his air shot sent him crashing to the floor. A Skyorl defender collected the ball and attacked once more.

'This is Total Football?' asked Gaux.

'No, sir,' said Nauton. 'This is total rubbish.'

'We're getting battered! What am I going to say at half-time?'

'Maybe you could work more on their Tic Tacs, sir?'

Phil bounced across his goalmouth, saving,

parrying, vomiting and blocking shot after shot.

'He's like a cat,' said Nick.

'I thought we were underdogs?' said a bemused Eddie.

The Earth United fans sang out loud: 'Mbappé saves, Mbappé saves!'

At home, Mr and Mrs Beatty beamed with pride. 'That's our son.'

'We know!' replied the gym.

Back at the match, Phil rolled the ball out to Sanjay. He pinged it to Nick, who ran down the line with it. Nick looked like he was about to cross it, but instead, attempted to do the Cruyff turn. His left leg missed the ball and he dragged back his right leg, knocking himself to the ground.

'That's our son,' said Mr Wilson.

'I know,' said Mrs Wilson.

A laughing Skyorl player took the ball and passed it up the pitch. The Skyorl team attacked again and shot for goal. Phil flew up, tipping the shot over the bar.

Sanjay ran over and slapped Phil on the back. 'You two are great.'

The Skyorl player taking the corner knew that if he kicked the ball anywhere near Phil, he'd bounce up and collect it. So he tried something new. He passed the ball to a player on the edge of the box. Phil read the play, and bounced from his goal, reaching the ball before the attacker. He smashed the ball away from his goal.

'He's our sweeper-shop goalkeeper!' screamed Nick.

Phil was breathless as the Ref blew for half-time. Earth United bounced their way off the pitch and into the changing room.

'Forget about Mbappé,' said Gaux, 'it turns out Beatty saves just as well. That was exceptional goalkeeping, Phil. As for the rest of you, what's the problem out there? You can't even keep the ball!'

'Well, to start with there are ten of them,' said a slightly concussed Sanjay.

'Do you know how hard it is to control? The pitch is shocking!' said Mia.

'She's right,' said Eddie. 'It's like playing on a trampoline.'

'I like it,' said Phil. 'Unfortunately, my stomach does not.'

'That's it!' yelled Nick. 'That's how we beat them! Eddie, remember last summer when we played on your trampoline?'

'Yeah,' said Eddie. 'You jumped off my garden shed to bounce me up into outer space!'

'Nerds,' said Mia.

'Well, that's what we do . . .' began Nick, and he laid out his plan.

The second half got underway. Nick passed the ball to Eddie. Sanjay set off, running around the approaching Skyorl players. They ignored him, rushing towards the ball and Eddie. They were almost upon him when Mia leapfrogged over Nick's back and landed right behind Eddie, bouncing him and the ball up into the air – into space! The approaching Skyorl players simply ran underneath him. On his way back down, Eddie passed the ball to Sanjay, who was all alone up the pitch. He took the ball, turned for goal, imagined his feet were game controllers and pressed *shoot* . . .

The Earth United fans went wild – they were one–nil up! Nick smiled. Their teamwork was paying off. For the first time, he thought, they were actually beginning to look like a real team.

'They always say the best players find space on the pitch,' said Pog. 'I've just never seen it forty feet up in the air before.'

'I agree,' said Lug, 'Earth United seem to have found a second-half bounce!'

Earth United continued with the plan, bouncing Eddie up into the air every time the Skyorls approached. Nick, Mia and Sanjay took turns leapfrogging over each other to send Eddie up into space. This gained them multiple shots at the goal, but they couldn't make any of them count.

It was Nick's turn to run around the approaching Skyorls – only this time, one of them turned back and followed him. On his way back down, Eddie passed to Nick. He was through on goal when the defender flew in and took him out. The Ref blew for a free kick on the edge of the Skyorls' box. Three Skyorl players lined up in a wall, but they were so skinny, they looked like a set of extra-long cricket stumps. Mia lined up the free kick. Nick whispered into her ear – she smiled and nodded. Nick ran towards the ball, and was just about to kick it . . . but at the last second, he bounced over it. The Skyorl cricket stumps jumped in anticipation of his strike. Right behind Nick came Mia, who toe-poked the ball along the ground, under the jumping wall and into the bottom right-hand corner of the net.

'Howzat!' screamed Mia.

Half the stadium went wild.

'Amazing free kick,' said Pog.

'They've obviously worked on that at the training ground,' added Lug.

'What was that?' screamed Gaux with delight.

'No idea, sir, they must've improvised,' said Nauton. 'But we're two–nil up with only thirty seconds remaining.'

The fourth official held up the board, to show how much injury time would be added. The crowd gasped, as the board showed twelve minutes.

'Where'd they get that from?' said Gaux.

'I don't know, sir. All my databanks will tell me is that it's Fergie Time.'[*]

The Skyorls were lifted by all the added time and went on the attack. Nick rushed towards the attacking player . . . as he did so, the player flung himself to the floor and rolled over more times than the National Lottery. The Ref blew for a Skyorl free kick.

'I never touched him!' said Nick.

On came the Skyorls' team doctor. He pulled out a can of cooling spray and applied it to the injured player's leg. The player jumped back up like nothing

---

[*] Fergie Time works outside the normal understanding of space and time. It is an imaginary number of minutes added to the end of a match to ensure a team wins, or at least draws.

had happened. They looked fresh as a daisy!

Mia stood next to Nick. 'It's funny how they pull out the magic spray and the player's suddenly fit and healthy again,' she said.

The Skyorls took their free kick and played it up the pitch, but as soon as Mia approached the player, he collapsed in a heap.

'They're faking injuries to free-kick their way up the pitch,' said Nauton.

'They're cheating, is what they're doing,' said Gaux.

The Skyorls continued to free-kick their way up the pitch until they were on the edge of the Earth's box. Nick hadn't seen this much diving since the last World Cup!

Nick and the others lined up in the wall. The Skyorl player shot for goal . . . and the ball looped over their heads. Even Phil's spring-heeled save couldn't stop it. The score was now two–one, with six added minutes still left to play.

'How can we run down the clock?' asked Mia.

'We take it to the corner,' replied Nick.

They kicked off, and Nick passed to Eddie, who

quickly ran to the left-hand corner of the pitch. The others rushed to join him. As the Skyorl team dashed towards the ball, Nick, Mia and Sanjay leapfrogged Eddie up into the air. The Skyorls could not get hold of the ball. Every time Eddie flew up, the Earth United fans screamed: 'Olé!' After another five minutes, and Eddie bouncing up to the heavens a further sixteen times, the Ref blew the final whistle.

'We're into the semi-finals!' screamed Gaux, turning to celebrate with Nauton – only to find he was not there. He'd bounced on to the pitch to celebrate with the team, his lights twirling and flashing. The Skyorls' manager reluctantly shook hands with Gaux, saying something in his own language that can't be repeated here.

# CHAPTER SIXTEEN

It was the morning of the semi-final and Gaux had some good news. 'You'll be glad to hear we're back to playing on grass.'

Everyone but Phil was happy. His bouncing-around-the-goalmouth days were over.

'Now for the bad news,' said Nauton. 'I've checked the weather forecast and it's predicted to rain.'

'Can you play in the rain?' asked Gaux.

Nick smiled. 'We're British! The rain's part of our heritage.'

'That's great,' said Gaux. 'Now, we need to get a

light training session in this morning. Trust me, we're playing the Sill-Qs – we need all the preparation we can get.'

The team all moaned and groaned as they once more crept in through the Grand Bigpuvian Hotel's service entrance. They quickly moved through the kitchens, turned into a hallway – and ran straight into two Bigpuvian hotel security guards.

'What are you lot doing in here?' growled one.

'Erm . . . run!' shouted Nick. The team dashed off, following Nick. The two guards set off after them in hot pursuit.

Nick and the others burst into the laundry room and dived into a trolley full of freshly laundered Sill-Qs football shirts.

As they all piled in, bodies landed on bodies.

'Your knee's in my face!' said Eddie.

'No. Your face is in my knee,' said Sanjay.

'There's no room,' said Phil.

'That's because you bring that stupid big backpack with you everywhere you go,' said Mia. She pushed Phil away and he slammed into Nauton. There was a gigantic *POP!* as Phil's backpack burst open, sending sweets all over the laundry trolley.

'No!' squealed Phil. He quickly began scooping up the treats. 'You owe me for the burst packets, Mia.'

'Is profit all you think about?'

'Those tickets to the cricket world cup aren't going to pay for themselves.'

'Sssh, they'll hear us!' whispered Nick.

'You're right,' said the security guard. 'We *can* hear you.'

Earth United's training session was over. The guards threw them all out of the back doors and into the street. The rest of the day was spent back at their hotel, going over the Sill-Qs' strengths (as they didn't appear to have any weaknesses).

That evening, they set off early for the stadium. However, everybody else must've had the same idea, as the roads were gridlocked.

'We're not going to make the kick-off,' moaned Gaux.

'Don't worry,' said the Illiot driver. 'I'll get us there!' He yanked on the wheel and flew off the main road down a side street.

The shortcut took them past an abandoned industrial estate, filled with makeshift homes and shelters. They were constructed out of pieces of cardboard and bits of old wood. Children of different alien races looked out from their humble homes as the cab sped by.

'Kids *live* here?' said Phil.

'All their parents are forced to work – it's Bigpuvian law,' said the driver. 'These kids will work one day soon as well.'

*If their parents are working, why do they live in such poverty?* thought Nick.

As the team drove by, hundreds of the alien kids ran from their shelters and cheered them.

A young Illiot brother and sister were holding up a handwritten sign saying: *Mbappé Saves!*

'Stop the taxi!' yelled Phil.

'Quick, before he's sick!' said Gaux.

The driver slammed on the brakes and the cab screeched to a halt.

'You OK, Phil?' asked Nick. 'Do you need to vomit?'

'No, this is a different kind of sickness – home-sickness. They remind me of my brother and sister,' he said, his voice filled with emotion. 'I can't believe I miss the little brats.' Phil got out, followed by the others. They were quickly surrounded by the alien kids, who all began to cheer for Earth United. Phil found his way to the two Illiot kids holding the sign. He unzipped his backpack and began giving them loads of sweets. They screamed with delight as he tossed chocolates, jellies, his profits – everything! He continued until his entire backpack was empty. To Nick, it looked as if a great weight had been lifted from Phil's shoulders as he watched the alien kids enjoy the treats.

Nick wrapped his arm around him. 'I thought Beatty saves?'

'Yeah, well, it's time Beatty gave.'

'What about the cricket world cup?' asked Mia.

'Who needs it?' said Phil, as a big smile appeared on his face. 'We're in the Galaxy one.'

'Erm, I'm sorry to spoil the moment,' said Gaux, 'but we do have a match to get to.'

They waved bye to the alien kids, jumped back into the taxi and flew off once more.

Back on Earth, the smelly old gym was a sell-out. The tension inside was building. This was going to be Earth United's toughest match yet. On the big screens the Quark Arena was filling up as the fans took their seats.

'We should be getting a cut of the gate,' grumbled the Welsh brothers.

'There's more important things to be thinking about,' said their mother.

'What, like Xboxes?'

'Like your sister, and what she's achieving.'

'Look!' said Mr Welsh. 'They're thinking about her.'

Up on the big screens, images of the alien fans beamed back. In the crowd, they had unfurled a gigantic flag with Mia's face on it. They all began to sing for Earth United.

'I can't believe that's our little girl!' said Mrs Welsh.

'I know!' said Mr Welsh. 'She's famous! And not

just world famous, she's Milky Way famous!'

Lucas Marshall and his Ernie's United teammates were handing out pegs to all the schoolchildren.

'What are you doing?' asked Mrs Hawn.

'It's for their noses, Miss. Earth United stink worse than this gym.'

Mrs Hawn's pink flamingo face turned red. She was just about to confiscate Lucas's pegs when one of the Welsh brothers said, 'Look, look! They're coming out!'

All eyes turned to the screens.

The Sill-Qs were coming out of the tunnel. The crowd cheered. They looked almost human, apart from their crimson skin.

'Wow. They look cool!' said another Welsh brother.

Then Earth United came out, and the crowd cheered even louder. 'The fans love them!' said Mrs Wilson.

Mr Wilson looked her in the eyes and took her hand in his. 'I know,' he said.

'When this is all over,' said Mrs Beatty, 'I don't think Phil's going to want to go back behind the counter again.'

Mr Beatty nodded in agreement. 'He's a star.'

'They're all stars,' said Eddie's grandma. 'And we should be proud of them. They didn't ask for any of this, but they're carrying the weight and expectation of the world on their shoulders.'

Mrs Singh looked at Mr Singh. 'And you said sports would be good for him. His back will be ruined!'

The Sill-Qs won the toss and kicked off. The gulf in class between the teams quickly became apparent: the Sill-Qs were exceptional. Their technical ability was of the highest order. Their passing was nothing short of magnificent, and their shooting was deadly. Phil was bombarded, and without the spring-heeled help of the Whey planet playing surface, his pitiful dives were far too short. The Sill-Qs soon had a two–nil lead.

In the commentary box, Pog and Lug had now put their support behind Earth United. They sat in matching replica Earth strips, but they weren't enjoying what they were watching.

'Sadly, I think Earth United have finally met their match,' said Pog.

Nick gathered the team together for a group huddle. 'We need to keep the score to at least two–nil till half-time.'

'How are we gonna do that? We're getting thrashed!' said Mia.

'Nick?' asked Phil, Sanjay and Eddie.

The team were looking to their captain once more – they were looking to Nick.

'We park the bus,' said Nick.

'I didn't even pass my cycling proficiency test! How are we going to drive a bus?' asked Eddie.

'No,' said Nick. '"Park the bus" means we sit back and defend.'

'What do you think we've been doing, all-out attack?'

'Listen,' said Nick, 'we sit back, double up on attackers, press them when they have the ball and defend the goal like our planet depends on it.'

They would've all gulped if they'd known how

true Nick's statement was.

They broke the huddle and Nick kicked off, restarting the match.

The Sill-Qs quickly won back the ball and charged forward once more. This time, however, they came up against . . . the bus. Nick blocked a shot with his chin, Eddie slid in to tackle a player, Mia headed cross after cross, Sanjay tried his best (but was constantly knocked over). They surrounded an attacking Sill-Qs player, hounding him until the player was forced to turn around and pass the ball back towards their own keeper. Earth United's blood, sweat and tears had paid off – the Ref blew for half-time, and the score was still two–nil.

The Earth United players collapsed into the changing room with exhaustion.

'I've got a stitch Frankenstein would be proud of,' said Eddie.

'My stitch has got a stitch,' said Sanjay.

'We can't keep that up – the bus is running on empty,' said Mia.

'We need help from above,' said Nick, holding his hands in prayer.

'I'll take help from below at this point,' said Phil.

Little did Nick know, his prayers would soon be answered.

The second half kicked off. The Sill-Qs won back the ball and were on the attack.

'One more goal and I think it's all over,' said Gaux, his face colour changing from green to grim grey.

The Sill-Qs were now breaking through the tired Earth defence. They hit the bar, then the post. A third goal seemed like just a matter of time. Earth United's fans in the stadium had given up on them, and the billions at home on Earth were resigned to their fate and had accepted defeat, when . . . a single drop of water landed on Nick's nose. The *rain* had arrived.

The Sill-Qs had broken through their defence once again – their striker was just about to unleash his shot – when the heavens opened, and rain poured down on the players. As the Sill-Qs' striker's foot moved to connect with the ball, his shirt exploded in an extravaganza of popping. The striker squealed and completely missed the ball.

Phil picked up the football and passed it to Sanjay. Sanjay pinged it to Eddie, who easily dodged around the Sill-Qs players and passed to Nick. The reason it was so easy was because the Sill-Qs were having a spot of bother. As the rain hit their shirts, all of them began to explode and pop! This caused the players to scream and jump and wriggle about. They no longer resembled a structured team, but looked more like a breakdance crew from the 1980s. Earth United simply passed their way up the pitch.

Gaux turned to Nauton, who was bewildered.

'Even I don't know how they're doing this one, sir.'

Nick sent the ball over to Mia, who blasted it past the exploding-shirt-wearing, body-popping Sill-Qs goalkeeper.

The scoreboard changed to two–one and the Earth United players celebrated.

The rain continued to fall. The Sill-Qs players' shirts were still popping and exploding; they just couldn't concentrate on the game. Nick nicked the ball as soon as they kicked back off. He crossed to Sanjay, who headed it into Eddie's path. Eddie slipped past the last defender and couldn't miss. The goalie's shirt was exploding more than ever – Eddie simply passed the ball into the net to make it two all.

Nick cheered and ran over to Gaux and Nauton to celebrate.

Gaux grabbed Nick by the shoulders. 'How on Bigpu are you doing this?'

'I haven't the foggiest idea! It must be something on their shirts reacting with the rain.'

Nauton's cogs cranked and twirled. 'I think it might have something to do with our failed training session this morning,' he said.

'Of course!' said Nick. 'When we dived into the laundry basket, Phil accidentally burst his seventeen packets of exploding popping candy. The candy must've covered their freshly washed footy shirts – and now they're reacting with this alien rain!'

As Nick was talking to Gaux, the Sill-Qs coach had called all his players to the sideline. Earth

United looked on in horror as the Sill-Qs players came back on to the pitch wearing fresh, clean shirts.

'Oh, no,' said Nick.

The Sill-Qs coach smiled and then turned to Gaux and Nauton. He held up the still-exploding shirts and shook his fists, giving them both a stern look.

'Maybe on their planet that's a friendly gesture, sir?' said Nauton.

On the pitch, the Sill-Qs were just about to restart the match.

'What now?' asked Mia.

'Park two buses?' suggested Nick.

'And a plane,' added Eddie.

The match resumed, but luckily for Earth United, even with their fresh shirts the Sill-Qs were not as good as they had been in the first half. The reason was once again the rain. On their home planet of Spad, all Sill-Qs football matches take place indoors. Therefore, playing in the rain was not ideal – they just weren't used to it. They still controlled the match, but their shooting was now wild and erratic, with shots flying high and wide.

Nick shouted to his players, 'Let's try and hold on! We could take this to a penalty shoot-out.'

'I don't like that idea,' groaned Phil.

The Sill-Qs had possession and were on the attack. Mia slid in and took the ball, but as she turned away, the Sill-Qs player grabbed the sleeve of her left arm and dragged her to the ground. Her shirt ripped as she fell. The Ref blew for a free kick and the Sill-Qs player was booked. The Sill-Qs player ran off, still carrying the torn remains of Mia's left sleeve.

'Oh, no,' whimpered Mia, who lay motionless on the ground, hiding her left arm.

The Ref signalled for the team doctor to come on to the pitch. Nauton clomped over and bent down. Nick stood over them, watching.

'What seems to be the problem?' asked Nauton.

'Go away!' yelled Mia, who had now drawn herself up into a ball.

'I can't. Not until I've assessed your injury.'

'I'm not injured,' said Mia.

Nauton stood up and whispered to Nick, 'Is this part of the game plan?'

Nick shook his head. This was not like Mia, he thought. She was tougher than the rest of the team put together. He bent down and gently whispered, 'Mia, what's wrong?'

Her tears fell on to the pitch. 'I just want to go home.'

'What happened?'

'That stupid player ripped the sleeve off my shirt. The top of my left arm is exposed.'

Nick couldn't see the problem – then he remembered. 'Mia, we're on the other side of the galaxy. Nobody cares if you have a tattoo.'

'It's not a tattoo,' said Mia. She lifted her right hand slightly off the top of her left arm and showed Nick what was underneath: a big, bright, purple birthmark. 'I hate it. People have been making fun of it my whole life. *Stain on society*, *freakshow*, I've heard it all. My brothers would use it as target practice, and the girls at my last school hounded me so much I had to leave. That's why, when I joined St Ernie's, I made up the story of the tattoo and kept everyone at arm's length. It's better that way. If I play on, everyone on Earth will see it – I'm gonna have to come off the pitch.'

'Hey, look at me,' said Nick. Mia did. 'There's nothing wrong with it. If others think that, they're wrong. That right there? That's nature's tattoo! Nobody else has one like yours. Be proud of it. Own it!'

'Easy to say when you don't have one.'

'Here, then.' Nick pulled the captain's armband off and handed it to Mia. 'Put this on. You're not going off – there's no team without you. You should be captain anyway.'

She pulled it up her arm – however, her birthmark was too large to be fully hidden, and showed around the edges.

The Ref rolled over. 'You do know when they say "do your talking on the pitch" that it's an expression, right? Are you playing?'

Mia got to her feet. She looked at Nick. 'I'm sorry.' She ran from the pitch, and down the tunnel.

'Is she coming back?' asked Eddie, coming over.

'I don't know,' replied Nick. Earth United were

now a player down.

Nick took the free kick and passed to Eddie, who passed to Sanjay, who kicked it back to Phil.

'What are they doing now?' said Gaux.

'Time-wasting, sir, it's perfect.'

The clock ticked down until there was only a minute left.

Nick had the ball; it was time to take it to the corner. He set off for the Sill-Qs' right-hand corner, but was tackled by a defender. She kicked the ball up to her teammate, who passed it on to the striker. There were only five seconds left. The Sill-Qs' striker swivelled with the ball and let fly with a right-foot pile-driver. The ball flew past the diving Phil and nestled into the top left-hand corner of the net. The Sill-Qs' fans went wild, and the Ref blew for full-time.

Three–two was the final score – Earth United were out of the cup!

Back on Earth, the whole planet was in mourning. In the gym, nobody except Lucas and his Ernie's United teammates could believe it.

'I knew those losers wouldn't win the cup,' said Lucas.

'They tried their best,' said Mrs Hawn.

'Well, their best has just cost us the Earth!' said Lucas. 'We might have stood a chance if *their* daughter hadn't run off the pitch.' He pointed to Mia's parents and then to Nick's. 'And *their* son had held on to the ball for the last minute of the game.' The gym fell silent. 'What? I told you they stink.'

One of his classmates threw a peg, and it bounced off Lucas's head.

'You're the one that stinks,' he said, and he began to boo him. The peg was followed by a scarf, then another and another.

'What's going on? I'm Lucas Marshall!' he said, cowering from the onslaught.

An avalanche of pegs, scarves and boos flew towards Lucas and his teammates.

The Earth United players sat in their changing room, deflated, depressed and defeated. They could hear the wild celebrations going on in the

Sill-Qs' changing room next door.

A tear-stained Mia stood up. 'I know you're all thinking it, so I'll just say it. We're out because of me. I shouldn't have left the pitch.'

'No,' said Nick. 'We play as a team, we lose as a team. It's all our faults.'

'You're wrong,' said Mia. 'I'm the reason. This is me saying, *Mia culpa*.'

Nick looked at her. 'Mia Welsh, was that a joke?'

'Tell anyone, and you all lose noses.'

Eddie raised his hand. 'I don't get it.' Mia started to giggle. This set Nick off, then Phil and Sanjay began to laugh.

'You think that's funny? When the resistance finds out what's happened, I'll be getting vaporized,' said a giggling Gaux. And with that, the whole team burst out laughing – they couldn't stop.

'Why are we laughing?' asked Nick, with tears streaming down his face.

Mia was howling with laughter. 'I have no idea.'

'I've got hiccups!' said Sanjay, through fits of giggles.

'I gave away all my sweets, my profits this quarter are going to be zero, and I still can't stop laughing!' said Phil.

'I still don't get it!' said Eddie.*

They were laughing so much that they never heard the celebrations from next door abruptly stop. They continued to laugh as an official representative from the GUFF entered their changing room.

'Can I have your attention, please?' said the official. The Earth United players continued to laugh.

'Excuse me, can I have your attention?'

The team ignored him, as they were now rolling on the floor.

'SILENCE!' yelled the official. All the team froze (curing Sanjay's hiccups) and stared at the small GUFF official standing before them.

'That's better,' he said. 'I'm here to let you all know the entire Sill-Qs team have failed their drug test. Therefore, they've been disqualified from the competition. Your team is now reinstated and are through to the final round. Thank you.' He turned

---

* *'Mea culpa'* is Latin for 'my fault'.

on his six heels and left.

There was a moment of complete silence. The team then erupted into celebrations of laughter, cheering and hugging one another.

# CHAPTER SEVENTEEN

Back at their hotel, they were about to watch the replay of the other semi-final: the Bigpuvians versus the Okuto.

Nick tapped Mia on the shoulder. 'Come on.'

'We're not watching the game?'

'We know who wins. I want to show you something.'

'Can't you show me here?'

'There's something I want you to see as well. It's at the Grand Bigpuvian Hotel. I noticed it last time we used their lift. I think you'll like it.'

Nick and Mia slipped away as the others settled

down to watch the match. Pretending to be paying guests, Nick and Mia strode into the Grand Bigpuvian Hotel once more. They entered the lift and Nick spotted the button he was looking for: *Viewing Platform*. He pressed it, and the lift shot off.

When the doors reopened, they were met with a building site. The room was circular in shape, the middle of which was filled with workbenches and building materials. The rest was still bare. It didn't matter – the view made up for everything. Gigantic windows ran around the outside of the room, giving an almost 360-degree panoramic view of the city – and it was magnificent. The city was lit up like a billion, trillion Christmas trees, the colours of which humans could only dream of. Flying cars flew in and around buildings of every shape, size and cost. The view was alive and thriving with energy. Mia pressed her face up to the glass.

'What do you see?' asked Nick.

'I see . . .' said Mia, 'money, power, beauty, greed, splendour, magnificence, hope. Why? What do you see?'

Nick pointed at her. 'Mia Welsh.'

Mia turned around.

'What a load of claptrap!' said Eddie, back at the Scrappy Hotel. The remaining teammates were huddled around Nauton's chest monitor, watching the game. Eddie was particularly unhappy with a refereeing decision made in favour of the Bigpuvian team, against their opponents, the Okuto. On the screen, Clawtic lined up a free kick. He ran and blasted the ball over the wall and into the goal.

'Wow,' said Sanjay. 'An absolutely amazing . . .'

'. . . player!' said Nick.

Mia frowned. 'No, I'm not.'

'You know me,' said Nick, 'I always state the obvious. And you know what else? I think Mia Welsh the angry tearaway might just be as much a fake identity as Alex Morgan was. You're more than that. You're Mia Welsh, the best teammate I could ever ask for – and a really great friend.'

Mia looked down at the floor. 'If you're trying

to build my confidence after what happened in the semi-final, thank you. But you don't have to worry, I'm OK. So, erm . . . was this what you wanted to show me? The view? Because it's . . .'

'Terrible,' howled Sanjay.

'I agree,' said Phil. 'The referee needs glasses! The Okuto should've had a penalty.'

'I think they're going to send him off for diving,' said Gaux.

'I can't believe it,' said Mia. Nick had lifted his sleeve to reveal a badly made sleeve tattoo – it tried to mimic Mia's birthmark, but looked more like a bruise. 'When did you get that made?'

'Just now. Lonky's made some for the whole team. Says it's something he does on the side.'

'I can tell,' said Mia. 'Why would you do that?'

'To show that we're a team. It's what team-mates do.'

Mia giggled. 'That's the worst tattoo I've ever seen, and my Uncle Geoffrey has one of a . . .'

\*

'Rhinoceros's bottom!' yelled Nauton.

'I must agree with you, my old rusting friend,' said Gaux. 'A lot of these decisions seem to be going the Bigpuvian team's way.'

Back on the top floor of the Bigpuvian Hotel, Nick said, 'Do you think our parents are missing us?'

'Not mine. They probably don't even know I've gone.'

'Really?'

'No, not really. They just don't have time for us. I know they do their best – they work, they have six mouths to feed after all. It's just . . .'

'Just what?' said Nick, encouraging her to continue.

'OK, you wanna know the real reason I smashed that window and got detention? I did it because for once I just wanted my parents to see me, you know?'

'I think the whole galaxy sees you now. Did you see the size of that last flag?' chuckled Nick.

Mia laughed. 'Right.'

'I have two home lives,' said Nick. 'My parents

are separated, I just wish . . .'

'They'd get back together?' asked Mia.

'Just getting along would be a start. Their constant fighting, it's exhausting.'

'Parents, eh? Who'd have them?' said Mia, smiling.

Nick was about to say something else when the lift pinged, and the doors opened. Nick and Mia dived into the centre of the room for cover, hiding behind a workbench. Nick thought it must be hotel security come to remove them from a restricted area – but he was wrong. Out of the lift walked Zaph, the Bigpuvian head coach, and by his side, in his floating hover chair, was Squirmo.

Back at the Scrappy Hotel, the replay of the game had finished. The Bigpuvians had won, five–nil.

'How on Earth United are we going to beat them?' asked Phil.

'Don't worry,' said Eddie, 'Nick and Mia will have a game plan.'

'Where *are* Nick and Mia?' asked Sanjay.

At that precise moment, Nick and Mia burst

into the room. Mia launched herself at Gaux.

'I'm gonna kill you!' she screamed.

Mia was dragged off Gaux by Nauton, Nick and the others.

'My goodness,' said a flustered Gaux. 'What in the universe's name is going on?'

'Tell them!' ordered Mia.

'Tell us what?' asked Eddie.

Mia stared straight into Gaux's eyes. 'Tell them about Clause 47.'

'Oh,' said Gaux. 'Who told you?'

'What's Clause 47?' asked Sanjay.

Nick spoke up. 'We've just heard an interesting conversation between Squirmo and Zaph about Clause 47, and what they're planning to do to our planet when we lose the final.' Nick threw dagger eyes towards Gaux. 'I *knew* there was something you weren't telling us.'

Phil put his hand up. 'I have no idea what anyone is talking about – will somebody please explain?'

'I think they have a right to know, sir,' said Nauton, looking at Gaux.

Gaux's face was changing to every colour of the rainbow. 'OK,' he said. 'I'll explain everything.'

'I *know* you will,' snarled Mia, fists at the ready.

Gaux took a deep breath; his face returned to its natural green and he began. 'Look at this planet – it's amazing, isn't it? The Bigpuvian people have everything. Well, before the Galaxy World Cup, this world was nothing – a stink hole at the back end of the galaxy. Then the tournament came along and changed everything. The Bigpuvians proved to be master footballers. As I've said, they've won every single Galaxy World Cup since its inception. And that's the thing – the tournament isn't just about football.'

'I know it isn't,' growled Mia.

'You see, once the Quillians had wormed their way to the top of every football federation, their leader, Squirmo, created the Galaxy World Cup. And, as head of the GUFF, he decided that the winners also get to conquer and rule the wildcard planet entry from each year's tournament.'

'Why would he add that rule?' said Phil.

'Greed,' said Gaux. 'The GUFF are so greedy,

they'd charge for a free kick if they could. The Quillians hate how they can't play in the tournament because of their lack of legs, so have secretly aligned themselves with the Bigpuvian team. So far, the Bigpuvians and the GUFF have conquered nine worlds, including Illioton and my home planet of Yossey, stripping them of every asset and enslaving their populations – it's how they and the GUFF are so rich.'

'No wonder those other alien and Illiot children are so poor,' said an angry Phil.

'Hang on,' said Eddie. '*We're* the wildcards this year.'

'Erm,' said Gaux. 'Yes, about that.'

'Do you mean if we don't beat the greatest team ever, Earth will be enslaved and stripped of all its assets?' asked Sanjay.

'Correct,' said Nick. 'It's why it's called the Galaxy *World* Cup. They literally win a world to rule over.'

'Gives you that extra incentive to win, doesn't it?' said Gaux, smiling weakly.

Mia sprang on top of Gaux once again. 'What

have you done? You picked us!' she squealed.

'I *suggested* you, there's a difference,' said a muffled Gaux.

Nauton came to Gaux's aid again, pulling Mia off him. 'Goodness, save your energy for the match.'

'Why didn't you tell us from the start?' said Eddie.

'When we abducted you, we thought we were getting the best players on the planet. I didn't want to saddle you with the extra pressure – I just wanted you to concentrate on your football, and win.'

'And now? Do you think we can still win?' said Nick.

'Well, I got Nauton to calculate our chances of victory . . .'

Nauton's cogs whirled. 'My databanks say, we have zero chance of success.'

The entire team launched themselves at Gaux.

# CHAPTER EiGHTEEN

The time leading up to the final seemed to take an eternity, but eventually the moment had come. The streets of Planet Earth were deserted. Every single soul was glued to a screen, waiting to discover the Earth's fate.

The smelly old gym hall was packed to capacity; the Welsh brothers had made a killing. The screens flickered to life and Pog and Lug (wearing their Earth shirts) appeared in the commentary box inside the luxurious Colossal Coliseum Stadium. The largest stadium in the galaxy, with one million seats – and every one was a sell-out. The screens showed the Bigpuvian president, Trulo, taking his seat in the executive area next to the delegates from the GUFF, including Squirmo.

Pog spoke: 'Welcome, viewers from around the Milky Way, to the tenth Galaxy World Cup final! The overwhelming favourites and undefeated Bigpuvians versus the wildcard underdogs, Earth United. What do you think the outcome will be, Lug?'

'Well, I've grown fond of these plucky little Earthlings these last two weeks, but I think this is one game too many. I just hope the score doesn't go to double figures. They don't deserve that.'

'I agree,' said Pog. 'It doesn't take a pair of Ultra-optic Lenses – sponsors of today's match – to see that Earth United have no chance.'

Inside Earth United's changing room, the atmosphere was flat. Nick looked at his teammates.

Sanjay was in denial: 'Maybe we could win, if we all play in goal?'

Mia was still angry: 'I just wanna take that stupid cup and ram it down their reptilian throats!'

Phil was trying to think around it: 'What if we offer them the moon instead – it might just work?'

Eddie had accepted defeat: 'Well . . . at least we came runners-up.'

Nick himself was in a deep depression: they were beaten, and he knew it.

A bruised Gaux (from his encounter with Mia) slowly stood up. 'I would just like to say that no matter what the outcome today, I'm proud of you and what you've achieved. You really shouldn't have made it this far, but you did – you beat everyone in your way. And now, because Nauton's rusty circuits say we can't win, do you give up? No! I wouldn't pick the real Messi, Ronaldo, Haaland, Mbappé or Morgan over any of you. You *are* Earth United. And when you people work together, you're the greatest team in the entire galaxy!'

Gaux's little speech stirred something inside Nick. He looked again at his teammates and his depression changed to pride, and then, most of all, hope. He stood up. 'Over the last two weeks, I've really got to know you all, and it's been the greatest experience of my life. We started out as strangers, then teammates, but what I see before me now are my friends. I've never had many friends, it was always just me and Eddie. So I'm not about to let my new friends down and lose to a bunch of crocodile wannabes. And I know my friends won't go down without a fight – we owe the Earth that much at least. What Gaux said is true: we're better when we all work together. We're better united!' Nick pulled on his sleeve tattoo. 'Now, who's with me?'

Phil stood up proudly next to Nick and pulled on his sleeve tattoo. 'Count me and my backpack in.'

Sanjay stood up next, rolling his tattoo up his arm. 'Me too. I'm never doing my homework again.'

Eddie (who was already wearing his tattoo) got to his feet. 'This is just like *Planet of the Apes*.'

'*No*, it isn't,' said Nick.

The teammates all looked at Mia. She slowly stood up and removed the captain's armband, leaving the bandage underneath to hide her birthmark. She held the armband out to Nick. 'You're wrong. You *are* the captain of this team.'

Nick shook his head. 'No, I'm just ordinary.'

'Close,' said Mia, 'you're actually *extra*ordinary.'

With a lump in his throat, Nick blinked back tears.

'My captain,' said Eddie.

'My captain,' said Sanjay and Phil.

'Our captain,' said Mia.

Nick felt ten feet tall. He took the armband and rolled it up his sleeve. Mia then began unwinding her arm bandage, until her birthmark was visible for the whole galaxy to see. 'Now, let's show the universe who we are, warts and all.'

'I have warts?' asked a bewildered Eddie.

'You *are* a wart!' yelled Gaux.

All the team cheered.

Gaux smiled at Nauton.

'I told you, sir, locker-room banter.'

'Let's win this for the Earth, for the Illiots, for the whole darn Milky Way!' shouted Nick.

Mia grabbed a big black marker pen. 'There's just one last thing we have to do . . .'

Back on Earth, in the gym hall, the parents, teachers and fans were discussing their team's chances of success. The answered ranged from:

'Zero!' (Lucas and his teammates.)

To:

'Of course we're going to win – they'll do it for the Earth!' (A stranger wearing a T-shirt with the slogan: *Save the planet!*)

'I'm sorry, who are you?' asked Mrs Hawn of the stranger.

'I'm Emma Chung. I'm Eddie's mum.' Emma spotted her own mum knitting in the corner and dashed over. Before anyone could say anything else, the fans inside the gym hall got their first glimpse of Earth United's opponents. The Bigpuvian team stepped out of the tunnel and on to the pitch.

'We need to start packing for the hills, now,' said Mrs Hawn.

Mr Barton fell to his knees and wept openly. 'It's all over.'

'Don't worry,' said Mrs Wilson, 'the cameras always add two feet and seven hundred pounds.' The entire Bigpuvian team towered over the Earth United players. Every single one of them was over seven feet. Their shirt size was awesome, covering bodies rippling with muscles. Their legs were as thick as tree trunks and their boots could crush tanks, for fun. Both teams lined up for the planetary anthems.

On the big screens in the smelly gym hall, Pog's eyes widened. 'Wait a minute,' he said. 'I don't recognize the names on the back of Earth United's shirts.'

'I've just been handed some information,' said Lug. 'Apparently we've had their names wrong for the entire tournament . . .'

The screens cut to the pitch as the Earth United team turned around to reveal their true names. On the back of their shirts, written in black marker pen, were: Wilson, Welsh, Beatty, Singh and Chung.

The families of the players were bursting with pride to see their names beamed out across the galaxy. Tears welled up in their eyes. They'd never been prouder of their kids.

\*

As the Earth United players got ready for their anthem to begin, the Bigpuvian players stood in a line in front of them. 'Shake It Off' began and the Bigpuvian players, led by Clawtic, began to do a ritual dance. They screamed and hollered and pushed their enormous jaws into the faces of their opponents. On the outside, Nick and the others stood proud, staring straight into the Bigpuvians' bright yellow eyes. On the inside, they were quaking with fear in their Bendy Boots. The Bigpuvian ritual lasted for the whole of the Earth's anthem, and finished with Clawtic standing directly in front of Mia.

'Hang on, I recognize you . . . Where from?' asked Clawtic.

'You don't remember?' said Mia. 'I'm the little ugly one that's gonna knock you out.'

Clawtic clicked his huge fingers. 'Autograph!' he laughed. 'No chance, Autograph – we're the greatest footballers ever. It'll be fun ruling over your ugly little species.'

The Bigpuvian players crossed their arms over their enormous chests as the planetary anthem of

Bigpu filled the arena. Once the anthem was complete, the Ref called over the two team captains. Nick's hand was shaking as he handed over the Earth's pennant. A proper flag, made especially for the final.* Clawtic snatched it off him, wiped his nose on it, scrunched it up and handed it back to Nick.

'Here's our gift,' laughed Clawtic.

Nick dropped the snot-covered pennant and it blew away in the wind. *Gaux's wallet won't be happy*, thought Nick. 'That cost a fortune.'

Nick won the coin toss and elected to kick off. He took the ball over to the centre circle, where Mia was waiting.

'What did he say?' asked Mia.

'He doesn't like our pennant,' said Nick, 'or us.'

Mia gulped. 'Hopefully we'll make it to half-time.'

'Hey, Autograph!' yelled Clawtic. 'Hurry up and kick off! We've a cup to win and a new planet to rule.'

Mia gritted her teeth and was about to march

---

* Unfortunately, Gaux had asked Phil's advice as to what best represented the Earth for their pennant. That is why Nick handed over a flag showing an image of a pickled onion crisp.

towards Clawtic but was pulled back by Nick. 'Ignore him, Mia, he's not worth it.'

The Ref's whistle blew, and Nick got the final of the Galaxy World Cup underway. Earth United's players soon found they had plenty of time on the ball. The Bigpuvian team were big and strong, but cumbersome. They were so slow, they couldn't get anywhere near the ball before the Earth's players passed it on. United played through the defence and Mia found herself in space, on the edge of the Bigpuvians' box. Nick slipped the ball to Sanjay, who flicked it on to Mia. A Bigpuvian ran up behind to challenge her.

'Alien on!' screamed Nick.

Mia heard Nick's call and dodged the tackle before unleashing a wicked shot for goal. The ball was heading in . . . until the keeper dived across her goal and caught it in her enormous jaws. She bit down, and the ball burst.

'What a save!' said Pog.

'Incredible,' added Lug. 'The Bigpuvian keeper has total control of her goalmouth.'

*

A new ball was sent on and the Bigpuvian keeper passed out to her defender. Mia jumped out of the way as they charged down the pitch.

Eddie looked at Nick. 'Mia doesn't get scared – that's our job.'

'Not any more! Get stuck in!' hollered Nick.

Clawtic had the ball and was on the attack. Eddie gulped and tried to tackle him. Clawtic slammed his forearm into Eddie's head, sending him tumbling across the pitch.

'Free kick!' screamed Gaux from the sideline, but the Ref was having none of it.

On the pitch, Nick and Sanjay ran together towards the approaching Clawtic. Their aim was to block off his run and somehow take the ball. They were just about to reach him when two other Bigpuvian players appeared on either side of them, crunching them together in a sandwich tackle. They were left in a heap on the floor.

'That's a sending off!' Gaux yelled at the Ref.

'I don't know, sir,' said Nauton. 'They seem to have been getting away with tackles like that for the whole tournament.'

Clawtic ran into the Earth's box and shot for goal. Phil dived to the left and the ball smacked off his right hand with an almighty crack!

'Aarrgggh!' howled Phil – but he'd saved the shot. The ball flew over the bar for a corner kick to the Bigpuvians.

The fans in the stadium cheered. 'Beatty saves! Beatty saves!'

'That was some save! Are you OK?' asked Mia.

Phil looked at his sore hand. 'Yes . . . but I'll never play the maracas again.'

The corner kick was taken, and the Bigpuvian players simply bashed the Earth players out of the way and into the back of the net. The ball landed on a Bigpuvian head, but she hit the ball over the bar and into the stands. The Ref blew the whistle.

'Finally,' said Gaux, 'a free kick goes our way.'

However, the Ref stunned everyone by pointing to the spot.

'A penalty for the Bigpuvians? I can't believe it,' said Lug.

'I think the Ref needs a pair of new Ultra-optic Lenses, available throughout the galaxy at all good Ghent stores,' added Pog.

The Earth United players surrounded the Ref.

'How can that be a penalty to them?' asked Nick.

'They flattened us!' said Eddie and Sanjay.

'You cheating tin can!' screamed Mia.

The Ref booked the entire Earth United team for dissent.

'I didn't even say anything,' grumbled Phil.

'They'll have to be careful now,' said Nauton. 'One wrong move and they're off, sir.'

'With this Ref, I don't think they stand a chance,' said Gaux.

Clawtic placed the ball on the penalty spot. He looked Phil in the eyes and roared at him, before stepping back a long, long way. Phil stood shaking in the middle of the goal. He couldn't move – fear had overtaken him. His legs were frozen to the spot. Clawtic charged towards the ball, then bashed it cleanly down the middle of the goal. The ball smashed into Phil's stomach, the force so powerful it carried the ball – and Phil – into the back of the net.

Clawtic ran past Mia to celebrate. 'One–nil! Did you like that, Autograph?'

With her nostrils flaring and teeth bared, Mia fixed her eyes on Clawtic and shouted, 'My name's not Autograph!'

The match restarted, and as soon as Earth United went on the attack, the Bigpuvian players flew straight in, kicking lumps out of them. The Earth's team were left in agony on the pitch.

'How is the Ref not seeing this?' asked Nauton.

'I don't know,' replied Gaux, 'but we should've had at least four free kicks.'

The Bigpuvians had the ball. One of their players attempted to do the Cruyff turn on Nick. He was so big and slow about it that he failed his Dutch driving test and came crashing down. The Ref blew his whistle for a Bigpuvian free kick.

For a brief heart-stopping second, Nick thought the Ref was going to show him another yellow, which would result in a red card and being sent off.

Luckily, the Ref just told him, 'Any more and you'll be off.'

Back on Earth, replays on the big screens showed Nick had never touched the Bigpuvian player.

'Don't they have VAR?' screamed Mrs Welsh.

'I think they do,' said Mrs Singh. 'Visually. Atrocious. Refereeing!'

Lucas, who hadn't uttered a word since the onslaught of pegs and scarves, spoke for the first time in days. 'They're cheating,' he said. 'It's not fair.'

'Mr Barton always says life's not fair,' said one of Lucas's teammates.

But Lucas was raging. He stunned his teammates by shouting, 'Come on, Earth United!'

The Bigpuvian defender launched the free kick into United's box. Clawtic towered over Nick and the others, and simply headed the ball past Phil and into the net. The score was now two–nil!

As the game approached half-time, United were on the attack once more.

'One, two!' shouted Eddie.

Nick kicked the ball to him and ran past the Bigpuvian player. Eddie returned the ball to Nick. He then ran up the pitch, yelling, 'Three, four!'

Nick again passed to him and dodged around the oncoming defender. Eddie once again passed straight back to Nick. Their teamwork had paid off – Nick was into the Bigpuvian box. The keeper rushed from her goal, but Nick simply slipped the ball to Sanjay. Sanjay was about to score when a Bigpuvian player jumped two-footed off the ground and into Sanjay's left leg. Sanjay flew into the air and landed flat on his back. His scream could be heard all the way back on Earth.

'That has to be a sending off!' screeched Gaux and the Singhs, from opposite sides of the galaxy. The Ref blew his whistle and gave the Bigpuvian team the free kick, saying that the ball had hit Sanjay's hand.

'It never touched his hand,' said Pog. 'The replay does not lie.'

'Yes,' said Lug, 'but maybe this referee does.'

\*

Nauton clomped on to the pitch, to see to the injured Sanjay. He looked at Sanjay's leg and didn't think the magic spray was going to help. His leg had snapped and was pointing the wrong way.

'Game over,' whimpered Sanjay.

Mrs Singh had had enough. She turned to her husband. 'First it was a concussion, then he was sandwiched between players, now it's a broken leg! *He needs to get out more*, you said, *he needs to play sports more*, you said. What he needs is a new computer! Sports are too violent.'

While Sanjay was tended to, the other Earth players huddled together.

'They're cheating us,' said Eddie.

'You mean the Ref is,' said Nick. 'He's giving them every decision.'

'Look, we just have to avoid them till half-time,' said Mia, looking over at Sanjay. 'We can't afford any more injuries.'

A team of Illiots stretchered Sanjay off the pitch.

Nauton walked over to Gaux and handed him Sanjay's shirt. 'His leg's broken, sir. You'll have to come on to replace him.'

'I'm not from Earth,' said Gaux.

'There's a clause which states if you've visited another world for more than ten minutes, and you've never played for another planet, then you are eligible to play for the planet you visited.'

'I can't play! I have two left feet, and I mean literally!' said Gaux, pointing down at his four feet.

'There's no one else, sir. I can't – robots aren't permitted to play.'

Gaux looked terrified.

'What's going on?' said Nick. 'Are you coming on?'

'I can't play! I'm terrible,' said Gaux.

Nick chuckled. 'We can't play either – you'll fit right in. How's Sanjay?'

'His leg's not good, but he'll be OK,' said Nauton. 'I will see to him.' Nauton stomped away down the tunnel.

Gaux squeezed into Sanjay's shirt and scuttled

on to the pitch.

The Bigpuvians took their free kick, launching the ball up to the halfway line. It landed at the four feet of Gaux. A second later and Gaux was flattened by Clawtic, who took the ball and went on the attack.

Meanwhile, Sanjay was on the treatment table. His leg had been straightened and was already in plaster.

'Thanks, Nauton. Now, I need one more thing,' said Sanjay. 'Can you get me to a computer terminal?'

If robots could smile, Nauton would have been grinning as he said, 'I can do better than that, sir. I am one.' A compartment opened on Nauton's belly. Inside was a keyboard and monitor. Sanjay sat up and began to type.

'What are you thinking, sir?'

'I'm just going to take a little look into our friend the referee,' said Sanjay.

# CHAPTER NINETEEN

Nauton and Sanjay were waiting in the changing room as the players hobbled in. Their plan to avoid the Bigpuvians till half-time had worked – they had no more injuries. Unfortunately, Phil couldn't avoid them, and had been forced into save after save. The list of instruments he'd never play again was now into double figures, but he'd stopped the goals. The score, amazingly, was still two–nil. Sanjay was about to speak, when behind him the changing room's toilet exploded to life.

'*Gaux!* Get in here!' screamed Lou.

Gaux and the team gathered around the toilet, its lights burning bright red.

'Erm, yes?' said Gaux.

'What in the moons of Cartheia is going on? Who in the blazes are these players? You lied to us! These are not Earth United!'

'You couldn't be more wrong,' said Gaux. 'I've never met a more united bunch than these kids. They help each other, they fight for one another. You hide in the shadows, but they're out there on the pitch giving their all to save their planet, and I am proud to be their manager.'

The whole team swelled with pride.

'That doesn't matter,' said Lou. 'They'll just be united in defeat . . . They're not good enough! You've ruined everything!'

'What was that?' said Mia. 'I'm sorry, we can't hear you.'

'Yeah, you're breaking up,' said Nick. 'The changing room's going through a tunnel.' Nick reached over and flushed the toilet. Lou's angry voice flushed away and the red lights faded. They left Lou and the toilet and moved back into the changing area.

'I have some news,' said Sanjay.

'Oh, Sanjay, sorry, how are you?' asked Nick.

'I'm fine . . . Listen, you're definitely going to believe this.'

Sanjay pointed to the monitor. 'The Ref's been hacked.'

'I knew it!' said Gaux.

'Are you sure?' asked Nick.

Sanjay nodded.

'That doesn't make sense. Why would the team that has the greatest player in the galaxy and who wins every Galaxy World Cup need to hack the Ref?'

'They're cheating,' said Eddie.

'I know,' said Nick. 'But why?'

'Well, I would cheat if I was rubbish,' said Eddie.

Mia looked straight at Nick. They both smiled and said, 'So that means, *they* must be rubbish!'

'You mean they've lied this whole time?' asked Gaux.

'Yes, they must be just as bad as us,' said Mia.

Nick turned to Sanjay. 'Can you re-hack the Ref

and put it in our favour?'

'Already tried to mod him, but it's beyond my level of knowledge – even Nauton can't do it.'

'Well, that's it,' said a resigned Gaux. 'There's nothing we can do. Lou's right – they've won.'

'Not yet,' said Mia. 'There's more than one way to hack a ref.'

Back on Planet Earth and with the team two–nil down, panic had taken hold. People were fleeing the major cities, stock markets were crashing, and the President of the USA was building walls around the White House. ('No aliens are getting in here.')

Everyone in the gym hall was deflated. They couldn't see a way back for Earth United.

Fans were giving up and leaving in droves. Then an unlikely source stepped up to try to halt the exodus.

'Where are you all going?' asked Lucas. 'Listen, I've been Earth United's harshest critic throughout the whole tournament, but you can't give up! I've seen enough from this team to know they can turn this around. Come on, we're Earth United, not

Earth Divided!'

The fans continued to leave.

'Call yourself fans?' said Lucas. 'Real fans don't desert their team. Real fans stick together through thick and thin. Real fans are united!'

The hall continued to empty.

Lucas ran up to the Earth United mascots (Mr and Mrs Wilson). 'Do something!' screamed Lucas.

Mr and Mrs Wilson held hands and, together, began to slowly sing Earth United's song:

'*United . . . we stand,*
*United . . . we fall,*
*United are the worst team we've seen*
*since Millwall.*
*Earth . . . United.*
*Earth . . . United.*'

The song returned to normal speed and the Singhs, Beattys and Chungs joined in:

'*We always stick together,*
*No matter who we face,*

*We'll never give up trying,*
*To save the human race.*
*Earth United!*
*Earth United!'*

The Welshes stood by their side, and sang their hearts out:

*'Even when we're losing,*
*We always have a plan,*
*We never stop believing,*
*We always say, "We can!"*
*Earth United!*
*Earth United!'*

Pretty soon, fans were dashing back into the gym and everyone, Lucas included, was singing along:

*'We'll sing it on the mountains,*
*We'll sing it in the street,*
*We'll sing it forever and always on repeat:*
*Earth United!*
*Earth United!'*

The news crews beamed the song out across the globe to fans in every home, street, village, town, city, county, state, country and continent. Everyone sang along, in all the beautiful languages of this amazing planet. For one brief moment, the Earth truly was **UNITED!**

# CHAPTER TWENTY

As the teams came out for the second half, Sanjay and Nauton stayed behind in the changing room. There was one more thing on the computer that Sanjay wanted to check.

The Ref blew the whistle and the Bigpuvians got the second half underway. The Earth United players all ran towards the ball. Then, at the last second, they all turned and kicked and hacked at the referee. The Robot Ref was sent flying into the air. It landed on its head and then burst into flames.

'Sorry,' said Mia. 'It was a complete accident.'

Zaph, the Bigpuvian head coach, looked on

with dismay, as the charred remains of the Ref were dragged from the pitch. A brand-new referee rolled up to the centre circle.

Gaux smiled. 'Now we'll see who *can't* play the best.' Nick looked at him in confusion. 'Don't worry, I know what I meant.'

The match restarted and the Bigpuvian team were on the attack. Nick slid in and tackled a player. He was about to run off with the ball, when he was grabbed around the neck and dragged to the ground. The Ref blew for a free kick . . . but this time the Ref gave the correct decision and it went Earth's way. The Ref then rolled up and booked the Bigpuvian player. The Earth United fans cheered at this, as much as if a goal had been scored.

'Let's get these goals!' screamed Nick as he took the free kick, booting the ball down the pitch.

The second half was a much more even contest. The Bigpuvians now knew they could no longer rely on a dodgy referee, so they had to play a straight game. This allowed Earth's players to get on the ball a lot more.

Phil threw the ball out to Mia. She jinked past

Clawtic and shimmied past another player. She had the goal in her sights. The Bigpuvian defence flew towards her, Mia lined up the shot and . . . PASSED!

'She passed!' said a stunned Pog, Lucas, Mrs Welsh, Gaux; in fact, everybody in the entire Milky Way!

A stunned Nick watched as the ball rolled over to his feet.

'Shoot, you idiot!' screamed Mia.

Nick instinctively shot for goal.

A wave of cheers, and Mia landing on him to celebrate, told him he had scored.

'Two–one!' said Lug.

'Earth United are back in the game,' said Pog.

Mr and Mrs Wilson jumped into each other's arms to celebrate – and kissed!

The Welsh brothers stood up tall and proud and sang:

*'M-i-a . . .*
*She plays without f-e-a-r . . .*

*She's worth her weight in g-o-l-d . . .
She's a player to be-h-o-l-d!'*

Nick couldn't believe it. 'You passed.'

'Yeah, it's what teammates do. It's what *friends* do,' said Mia.

The Bigpuvians kicked off, but somehow managed to put it out for an Earth throw-in. Mia took the throw, launching the ball down the wing to Nick. Nick dummied the ball past one player, then turned inside another. He passed to Gaux, who was standing alone in the box. Gaux tried to work out his feet and completely missed the ball, which rolled into the Bigpuvian keeper's hands. The keeper laughed at Gaux and he turned away in embarrassment. A moment later, and Gaux was on the ground and the ball was in the back of the net. The fans were going wild. Mia and Nick jumped on top of him – and the score was now two–two.

'I think we've just seen the worst goal of all time!' said Pog.

The replay showed the Bigpuvian keeper's

attempt to kick the ball down the pitch. It had never got that far. Instead, it had bounced off the back of Gaux's head. The ball had looped up over the keeper and into the net.

'I knew your big head would come in handy,' said Nick.

'I did tell you this was a game for using the brain,' said Gaux.

The Ref blew their whistle to restart the match, and a moment later, blew for full-time. The game was going to extra time.

Sanjay and Nauton had come back out pitchside just in time to see the equalizing goal.

Extra time kicked off and it was a sight to make eyes sore, especially with Ultra-optic Lenses. Both teams looked shattered. It was so slow and boring that it felt like extra-extra time. There was not one single shot on target in the whole first half.

The second half of extra time got underway, and Mia and Nick were on the attack. Clawtic rushed up to meet them.

'Hey, Autograph? You and your little friend here

will make nice slaves when this is all over.'

Nick had had enough of Clawtic's bullying. It was time to take a stand. It was time to become the Nick Wilson outside the window. He took aim and blasted the ball off Clawtic. 'Her name's not *Autograph*! How would you like it if I called you – Clawtickle!'

Clawtic stopped dead. 'What did you say?'

'Clawtickle. It's not nice being called names, is it?'

Word quickly spread around the ground and the fans began to laugh. The chant of 'Clawtickle' rang out around the stadium.

'My name's Clawtic!' raged Clawtickle.

'The fans seem to think differently,' said Mia.

Clawtic wasn't as thick-skinned as he looked. He snapped, grabbing Nick in one of his ginormous claws.

Zaph, the Bigpuvian head coach, screamed from the dugout: 'You'll get sent off, you fool! We need you on the pitch to score the winning penalty.' He looked at the rest of the team. 'Help him.'

The other Bigpuvian players responded by freeing

Nick and pulling Clawtic away to their end of the pitch.

Mia helped Nick to his feet. 'You OK?'

Nick did a quick check to be sure, then nodded.

As the Ref rolled over to Clawtic, the United fans all began to sing (to the tune of Earth's planetary anthem), 'Send him off, send him off!' Unfortunately, the Ref only gave him a yellow card. It was the first booking of his career.

'One more card and Clawtic's off,' said Nick.

Zaph obviously realized this as well and screamed a new set of orders at his team.

The game restarted with an Earth United free kick. Nick passed back to Mia, who stood on the ball. 'Why aren't they coming to get the ball?' she asked. The Bigpuvians were standing around the centre circle, just staring at Nick and the others.

'They're playing for penalties,' said Nick. 'Attack!'

Mia ran up the pitch towards the Bigpuvians. She tried to slip the ball through to Eddie, but Clawtic intercepted it. However, instead of going on the attack, Clawtic passed it all the way back to his goalkeeper. They then formed a green wall around the keeper.

'What do we do?' asked Mia.

'We try and break through,' said Nick. But Nick and the others found it impossible – the green wall was impenetrable.

The final minute ticked away and the Ref blew to end the match. The game was going to penalties!

# CHAPTER TWENTY-ONE

The Earth United players came to the side of the pitch and huddled up. 'Quick, we need a plan,' said Nick. 'Isn't Clawtic supposed to be brilliant at taking penalties?'

'He's right,' said Gaux. 'Clawtic's never missed.'

'What do we do?' said Nick. 'We can't get this far and fail now.'

Blank faces stared back at him until Phil stepped forward. He unzipped his (restocked) backpack and pulled out a Flompa Wompa bar. 'It's time to take one for the team,' he said.

'Wait!' said Nick, but it was too late. Phil

unwrapped the bar, tossed it in his mouth and swallowed.

Three seconds later, his transformation began. His forehead expanded outwards and his cheeks ballooned up, making him look like a jazz trumpet player on their busiest night. His right leg swelled up to twice its original size (his left leg, weirdly, remained the same). Most importantly, however, his hands began to grow. They swelled up and up and up, and because the Give 'n' Take Gloves were made of flexi-fabric, they grew too. Phil's gloves now resembled two gigantic snow-shovels. With hands that big, he could literally save the planet.

The Ref blew, instructing both keepers to head towards the designated goalmouth. The Bigpuvian team had won the toss and selected their fans' end of the ground. A chorus of boos greeted Phil as he slowly moved towards the goal, dragging his swollen right leg behind him.

'I don't know *what* has happened to Earth's keeper,' said Pog.

'He seems to have been given a helping hand . . .

Their chances of success have definitely grown,' said Lug.

'What have they done to our son?' asked a horrified Mrs Beatty.

'Well,' said Mr Beatty, 'you always said he needed to fill out.'

Lucas began clapping his hands and shouting, 'Beatty saves! Beatty saves!'

Others took up the chant, and soon the whole gym was cheering, 'Beatty saves!'

The Bigpuvian team had chosen to take the first penalty kick. Phil slowly moved to the goal line. He turned to face Clawtic. Clawtic smiled, revealing razor-sharp teeth, and growled at Phil: 'The bigger your hands, the bigger the mess when I blast the ball straight through them.'

'You're wrong,' said Phil. 'Haven't you heard? Beatty saves.'

The chant of 'Beatty saves!' was now coming from the Earth United end of the stadium. Phil stared down Clawtic, but his face continued to swell. It was so bad now that his eyes had closed –

he could see nothing. 'Oh, *Sherbert Dip Dab*,' he said.

Clawtic took ten enormous steps back and then sprinted towards the ball. Phil could hear him running. He counted down from three and blindly dived to the right, snow-shovel hands outstretched. The furious shot blasted off his right hand; he'd never play the glockenspiel again. There was a moment of silence as he crashed to the ground, then wild screams from the fans on the other side of the stadium.

'I saved it!' screamed Phil, who climbed to his feet and was immediately flattened by his celebrating teammates.

'I don't believe it, Clawtic can't believe it – he's missed a penalty!' said Lug. 'But you won't miss with Ultra-optic Lenses.'

'Incredible,' said Pog. 'If the Earth score their penalty, they win. The pressure on this next kick will be enormous. The fate of their entire planet depends on it.'

*

Gaux nervously smiled. 'Who wants to take the penalty?'

'I can't – I'm blind,' said Phil.

Gaux shook his head. 'I can't do it. I'm no good in high-pressure situations.'

'I'm no good in *any* situation,' said Eddie.

That left either Mia or Nick. They looked at each other and both said, 'I'll do it.'

'No, seriously, I'll do it,' said Nick.

'If you miss, the whole planet will blame you. Let me do it – the world doesn't like me anyway.'

'*We* like you,' said Nick, and the rest of the team agreed.

Mia blushed. 'If you do, then let me take it.'

Nick shook his head.

'OK, but before you kick the ball . . .' Mia gestured for Nick to come in closer. It looked like she was going to whisper something to him. Then Mia punched him in the face. 'Sorry,' she said as Nick fell over. Mia grabbed the ball and ran off towards the goal.

Nick was pulled to his feet. He rubbed at his new black eye. 'Wow. I guess she *is* the best striker.'

Mia passed the Bigpuvian team on her way to the goalmouth.

'Don't worry, team,' said Clawtic. 'They've got Autograph taking it. She's so ugly the ball will be scared and move out of the way.'

Mia ignored him and confidently placed the ball on the penalty spot. She stepped four paces back, readying herself to shoot.

The crowd held their breath.

The entire population of Planet Earth held their breath.

'I can't watch,' said Phil. 'Literally.'

Eddie couldn't watch either. He turned to look at the Bigpuvians' bench. Zaph was frantically signalling to someone in the crowd.

Mia ran up to the ball. She was about to strike it, when the ball moved – and she landed flat on her back.

'Told you,' said Clawtic, laughing.

'What happened there?' asked Nick. Mia got to her feet and mouthed something towards the bench. 'She's too far away.'

'Here, sir,' said Nauton, as he handed Nick a

pair of Ultra-optic Lenses.

'Where'd you get these?'

'We were presented with a pair – they're sponsors of today's match.'

Putting them on, everything became clear for Nick, as he could now read Mia's lips. 'She says the ball moved by itself.'

'Impossible,' said Gaux. 'Unless . . .'

'What?' screamed Nick.

'It can only mean one thing – *mind control*. Somebody is manipulating the ball.'

'I think I know who,' said Eddie. He had followed Zaph's signalling, and it led all the way to the GUFF in the executive area, at the other side of the pitch.

'Squirmo, of course,' said Gaux.

They all looked towards the executive area . . . and there was Squirmo. He had one hand to his enormous head and the other outstretched towards the pitch – and Mia's ball.

'If she shoots now, Squirmo will control the ball, Mia will miss, the Bigpuvians will win and Earth will be doomed,' said Nick.

'Wow,' said Gaux. 'Mia's right, you really do state the obvious.'

'How can we stop him?' asked Eddie.

'He's too far away and Mia's about to take her kick,' said Sanjay.

'Get me a ball!' ordered Nick.

The Ref blew the whistle. Mia eyed the keeper and then the ball.

Eddie dropped a ball at Nick's feet. Nick looked off towards the executive area and his mind went into overdrive. To get the ball there, he'd need to bend it off the corner flag at a precise angle using the golden ratio divided by the Fibonacci sequence. He couldn't believe it – he was actually using science and maths. Maybe there *was* something to this schoolwork. Maybe it wasn't boring after all. Like the windows in school, he'd have to look into it.

Nick and Mia took several steps back. They both ran towards their balls, striking them at the exact same moment.

Time is relative.

Nick's ball flew off towards the corner flag.

\*

Back on Earth, they watched as Mia hit her ball. Time seemed to slow down as the ball crept slowly towards the Bigpuvians' goal – in slow motion!

Mrs Hawn looked at Mr Barton. 'Isn't it meant to go faster?'

As Mia's ball continued its slow journey towards the open arms of the smiling Bigpuvian keeper, Nick's ball hit the corner flag, bouncing off towards the empty goal. It struck the bar and spun up into the crowd, hitting two Earth United fans before zipping up and smashing off the commentary box. It flew back down into the executive area and landed squarely on Squirmo's head – knocking him flat out!

The psychic link was broken. Mia's ball returned to normal speed, catching the Bigpuvian keeper unawares. It flew past her, on its way to bursting through the net!

The Bigpuvian fans fell to their knees. They couldn't believe it.

As for everyone else, a noise equal to the original Big Bang could be heard from one side of the

Milky Way to the other, as they celebrated the winning goal.

'They've done it!' squealed Lug and Pog as they leapt into each other's arms.

The Earth was saved! All the humans jumped as one to celebrate, causing a tidal wave so big, it swept across the entire planet, sweeping up the litter-filled streets and cleaning out the filthy hallways of FIFA. The Earth had never looked so good.

'Now, this is just like *Guardians of the Galaxy*,' said Eddie.

'No, it isn't,' said Nick, as the Earth United team ran on to the pitch (Sanjay hobbled), screaming with delight, and dived on top of Mia.

Led by Clawtic, the Bigpuvian players surrounded the Ref and demanded the penalty be retaken.

From under the mass of bodies, Nick could see what was happening. 'They're still trying to cheat.'

'Not for much longer,' said Sanjay, who signalled to Nauton.

Nauton's cogs twirled and buttons beeped. 'Signal and message sent, sir.'

On the big screen inside the stadium, Zaph and Squirmo appeared. The same image was now being broadcast across the galaxy on every wavelength and frequency.

The Referee's body camera showed Zaph and Squirmo in the Ref's chambers. Spare parts and other offline Robotics Refs filled the room.

Zaph spoke first, looking directly down the camera. 'Are you sure the referee has been hacked in our favour?'

'Don't worry,' answered Squirmo. 'Every refereeing decision will go your way.'

'And if we still aren't winning?'

'My mind control will take care of the rest, you know this.'

'I like to double-check.'

'Have I ever let you down in the past?'

'No.'

'Exactly. Do you think your stupid big bunch of lumbering reptiles could've won any of their Galaxy World Cups without my mind control help? Of course not. I've fixed this whole thing since the very first tournament. None of your wealth and fame would've been possible without me. Now, I'll concentrate on my end – you just get your team to look like they can play football.'

The footage ended with: *This message was brought to you by Singhster456!*

'That's our son,' said the Singhs, beaming with pride.

'We know,' said the gym.

On the pitch, the Bigpuvian players fell to their knees. They knew it was all over.

The entire stadium was in shock.

The entire galaxy was in shock.

There was complete silence as everyone digested the information. The Bigpuvians had fixed every Galaxy World Cup. This meant they were disqualified – and all the previous cups were void.

Gaux started to chant: 'Free the planets!'

The chant was taken up by the whole Earth United team. 'Free the planets! Free the planets!'

Soon the whole stadium and fans across the galaxy had taken up the chant.

'Free the planets! Free the planets!'

Trulo, the Bigpuvian president, marched on to the pitch, surrounded by his security team. A mic was handed to him.

'As president of the Bigpuvian people, I can say with hand on my hearts that we knew nothing of this betrayal. I hereby free all the planets under the rule of Clause 47, and ban the clause altogether from future tournaments.'

The stadium went wild with delight.

The galaxy went wilder with delight.

'Earth United have not only won the cup, they've also freed the enslaved planets and saved the Milky Way,' said Pog.

'Unbelievable,' added Lug. 'And all sponsored by Ultra-optic Lenses, where truth and justice become clear.'

The fans in the stadium turned their singing towards Zaph:

*'You're getting vaporized in the morn-ing!*
*Vaporized in the morning,*
*Vaporized in the morn-ing,*
*You're getting vaporized in the morning.'*

Zaph quickly dashed away and down the tunnel. Squirmo had already disappeared from the executive area.

Clawtic was still on his knees as Mia approached him.

'Autograph,' whimpered Clawtic.

'OK,' said Mia, as she pulled out the marker pen and scrawled her autograph across his head. 'There,' she said, 'you're just as pathetic as before.'

A stage was hastily erected in the centre of the pitch and the Galaxy World Cup was brought out. But first, Trulo handed out the award for player of the match.

Mia's face lit up as her name was read out. She collected her award – a golden Bendy Boot – and said, 'I share this award with my Earth United teammates and coaches. Who've shown me that no matter what we come up against, together, we can defeat it.'

The whole team walked on to the stage. Trulo picked up the Galaxy World Cup and passed it over to Nick. The cup was magnificent, with a gleaming diamond base featuring hands of creatures from across the galaxy reaching up to form a titanium column, which held a golden football surrounded by a jewel-encrusted spiral Milky Way. As one, the Earth United team lifted the trophy up. Fireworks exploded around the ground and confetti rained down. The fans in the stadium went wild, cheering, clapping and singing the name of Earth United.

The players ran to all sides of the arena and applauded the fans in return. They grabbed hold of Gaux and threw him up into the air to celebrate. They took a pitchside ice bucket and poured it over Nauton's head. His circuits fizzed and buzzed, and he lost six years of memories, but it was worth it. Earth United were the champions of the Milky Way.

# CHAPTER TWENTY-TWO

Lonky wept as Nick and the team left the Scrappy Hotel for the final time. He'd never had guests stay so long! Nauton flagged down a passing hover cab and everyone got in. As they pulled away, the doors of the Grand Bigpuvian Hotel burst open behind them.

Nick looked back to see hundreds of Illiot workers spill out on to the street. There were bellhops, waiters, cooks, cleaners and more. 'What's going on?' Nick asked.

'They're all going home,' said the cab driver, his voice sounding familiar. 'And I'll be joining them –

you're my final fare. Let's see the Bigpuvians run this place without us,' he laughed.

Nick now realized who the voice belonged to. 'Lou!'

Lou winked at Nick in the rear-view mirror.

'You're the resistance?' asked Mia.

'Of course,' said Nick. 'The resistance has eyes and ears everywhere . . . The Illiot workers, brilliant!'

'And nobody notices us,' said Lou.

Gaux gulped. 'Lou, I can explain . . . there was a mix-up on Earth and . . .'

'No need,' said Lou, interrupting him. 'Your team has not only broken the Bigpuvians' stranglehold over the tournament, but freed all the enslaved planets.'

'What will happen to the Bigpuvians?' asked Nick.

'I imagine that every enslaved planet will now sue the Bigpuvian Empire in the galactic high courts. Their reign is over. Everyone's wealth and resources will be returned, and it's all down to you. They'll build statues of you across the Milky Way.'

'Wow,' said Nick. 'And to think, Mrs Hawn said we wouldn't accomplish anything in the world.'

'She was sort of right,' said Eddie. 'After all, this is Bigpu.'

'I hope when they build the statue it will look like me *before* I ate the Flompa Wompa bar,' said Phil.

'And as for you, Gaux and Nauton . . . The resistance would like to present you with their highest honour.' Lou passed back two small tubes.

Gaux opened one and pulled out a rolled-up parchment. 'We have officially been made honorary free citizens of Planet Illioton.'

'What does that mean, sir?' asked Nauton.

'It means,' said Lou, 'that if you ever visit our planet, everything there is free.'

'Wow,' said Gaux. 'Thank you. This is a tremendous honour.'

Phil whispered into Nick's ear, 'How come they get free stuff and we get some dodgy statues we'll never see?'

The taxi pulled up outside the spaceport.

'How much do we owe?' asked Nick.

'No charge,' said Lou. 'This one's free, just like

my home world.' The team got out. 'So long, Earth United. You've made an old Illiot very happy.' Lou beeped his horn in triumph and drove away.

'Does anybody else want to carry the trophy now?' asked Sanjay. 'I can't feel my arms.' Nauton took the trophy off him and they headed into the spaceport.

Inside, Eddie still couldn't comprehend what had just happened.

'No, Eddie,' said Nick, 'the toilet wasn't driving the taxi. It was . . .'

But before Nick could explain further, he noticed hundreds of aliens gravitating towards them. A million selfies and autographs later, and the team made it through the spaceport, past customs and back on to the *Messenger*. With their luggage and Galaxy World Cup safely stored away, they all made their way to the central chamber.

Nick looked at everyone. 'I can't believe it . . . it's finally starting to sink in. We actually won!'

'We can't believe it either,' said a cold voice. A hidden compartment in the wall had popped open, and out of it crawled Zaph, followed by the floating-chaired Squirmo. Each was holding the latest XTC laser gun. They pointed the weapons towards Nick and the others, forcing them back into the upright tables. Straps wrapped around them; the entire team was trapped.

'You've ruined everything,' said Squirmo.

'You lied and cheated,' said Nick.

'And you didn't? You weren't even the real players!'

'We didn't enslave any planets,' said Mia.

'Yeah, we only lied to survive,' added Eddie.

'I knew it,' said Zaph. 'They *did* lie.'

'Way to go, Eddie,' said Phil.

'The universe will know about this,' said Zaph. 'We'll demand a replay.'

'Forget that,' said Squirmo. He held up the gun. 'Earth United are about to have an unfortunate accident.' He pointed the gun towards Sanjay. 'Now, where is the Galaxy World Cup?'

'Erm . . . my nana ate it,' said Sanjay, as he winked at Eddie.

'Enough of their lies!' screamed Zaph. 'Shoot them.'

Nauton's control panel beeped. 'We're coming up on the wormhole, sir.'

'You know what to do,' said Gaux.

Before Squirmo and Zaph had time to react, a door in the floor opened and they were sucked out into the cold vacuum of space. The door closed and everyone breathed a sigh of relief.

'What just happened?' asked Mia.

'We always dump our rubbish before entering the wormhole,' said Nauton.

# CHAPTER TWENTY-THREE

Back on Earth and the entire town of Hebbrow had turned out to welcome home their galactic heroes. The streets around the school were jam-packed with banners, bunting, flags and people. The park was full – the ducks had never eaten so much in their lives. There was a carnival atmosphere as everyone awaited Earth United's arrival.

The playground at St Ernie's had been marked out as a landing site, and news crews from around the globe had turned up to witness their return. They and the entire school's pupils and staff were looking to the skies.

'Here they come,' said Mrs Hawn.

The school's band struck up an out-of-tune version of Queen's 'We Are the Champions' as the *Messenger* descended from the clouds and landed perfectly in the playground. Eddie's grandma's hand-knitted red carpet was rolled out as the door hissed open and fell forward to create a gangplank. Out of the mist came Nick, Mia, Sanjay, Eddie and Phil, all wearing their Earth United football strips and winners' medals. They were followed by Gaux and Nauton. The crowds – many of whom were wearing replica Earth United strips – went wild.

Gaux looked at the cheering crowds. 'They adore us, Nauton.'

'I agree, sir. Maybe we should present them with a gift.'

Gaux searched inside his bag and pulled out his pair of Ultra-optic Lenses. He threw them up into the crowd. They were caught by the old couple who usually fed the ducks. They would now have the best eyesight in England.

The Ernie's United players and Mr Barton

formed a guard of honour as Nick and the others left the ship. Lucas and the rest of Ernie's United held up their right hands to their foreheads. With their thumbs stuck out and index fingers raised they all formed the letter 'L', then, as one, shouted, 'Legends!' The crowds cheered even more.

Nick looked at Lucas, who dropped his right hand from his forehead and held it out. Nick shook Lucas's hand.

'I'm sorry . . . friends?' asked Lucas.

'Friends,' said Nick.

'Now, how about a rematch?' said Mia.

'No. No way,' said Lucas, shaking his head. 'We're not playing the best team in the galaxy.'

The team walked on and up on to a raised platform that the local council had erected for them.

Everyone was there: classmates, the King, the President of the USA, and scouts from all the big teams, including Real Madrid, Bayern Munich and Sunderland. Even the real Ronaldo, Messi, Morgan, Haaland and Mbappé had turned up.

Nick spotted hundreds of fans wearing fake sleeve tattoos in solidarity with Mia. 'Look,' he said and pointed towards them. Mia welled up as she saw people celebrating her birthmark.

'It feels better than winning the cup!' she said.

'This is so cool!' said Sanjay, and the rest of the team agreed.

Their parents, carrying their huge Earth Re-United banner, rushed on to the platform to join them.

'Gran!' screamed Eddie. He dashed over and bent down to plant kiss after kiss on his grandma. 'I've been to space!'

'I know,' said Emma.

Eddie looked up. 'MUM!' He flew into her arms.

Tears flowed from his mum's eyes. 'I go off to save the planet and you do one better and save the galaxy! Well, I'm done trying to save the Earth – time I focused on you for a change.' Eddie's face lit up.

Phil's mother and father smothered him in a great big hug. 'My little boy,' Mrs Beatty said. (Phil towered over her.)

'I've missed you all so much,' said Phil. A thousand kisses later, and Phil was released.

'Oh, my goodness,' Mrs Beatty said. 'What is all this mess on your shirt, that's now all over me?'

'That's his vomit,' said Mr Beatty.

Phil grabbed hold of his younger brother and sister and told them how much he loved them. They stepped back, looking confused – they weren't used to their big brother being so nice. He unzipped his backpack and handed over a handful of alien sweets.

They snatched them up, and both said, 'Erm, so, about your room . . .'

'What have you done?'

Sanjay's parents almost flattened him as they picked him up and swung him around.

'Watch my leg!' screamed Sanjay.

The Singhs signed Sanjay's leg cast and his mum whispered, 'You are never leaving the house again.'

Mr Singh presented Sanjay with a huge wrapped box. Sanjay ripped it open to reveal the latest ultra-powerful gaming PC. A big smile broke across his face. He was already planning to write a computer game based on their adventure. 'I'm back!' said Singhster456.

Mia's family broke down as she rushed to greet them.

'We can't believe what you've achieved . . . We're so proud of you,' said her tear-stained parents.

'Yeah, sis,' said her brothers. 'You showed those aliens what for.'

They formed a circle around Mia and all began to sing Mia's football song. Mia couldn't stop crying. She pulled out her golden Bendy Boot and gave it to her brothers. 'You can sell this,' she said. 'New Xboxes all round!' The Welsh brothers burst into tears.

'There seems to be an awful lot of crying for such a happy occasion,' said Gaux.

'Well,' said Nauton, 'they are a water planet, after all.'

Nick noticed his parents were not only crying, as they dashed towards him, but were holding hands! They wrapped their arms around him in a circle of love. 'We thought we'd never see you again.'

He looked at them strangely. 'Are you two getting along?'

'This whole experience has made us realize how much we love you and each other,' said his mum.

'We're better united,' said his dad. Mr and Mrs Wilson then kissed.

'That's disgusting,' Nick said, but inside he was glowing.

Mrs Hawn stepped on to the platform. 'I just need a quick word with the pupils,' she said. She pulled the group to one side. 'Just because you saved the galaxy doesn't mean you're getting out of detention. I expect to see you all there tomorrow, no excuses.'

'We definitely will, Mrs Hawn,' said Nick. 'Putting us in detention is the best thing that's ever happened to us. We travelled to the other side of the stars, won the Galaxy World Cup, and saved Earth from Bigpuvian slavery. And I made the best bunch of friends in the galaxy. Plus, this whole experience has taught me a valuable lesson.'

'And what's that, Mr Wilson?'

'Saturn.'

'What about Saturn?'

'You mean, you don't know?'

'Know what?'

'It's the sixth planet from the sun, Miss.'

'Never mind that – what other things have you seen? You must tell me. The benefits towards our scientific knowledge could be astronomical. Nick Wilson, are you even listening to me?'

Nick wasn't. He was looking at his family and friends. Nothing else mattered, only them.

Nauton and Gaux brought out the Galaxy World Cup and passed it over to the team. As one, they lifted it up and everyone went wild with joy – even Mrs Hawn.

'Hey, Eddie,' said Nick. 'This would make a great ending if they ever made our story into a movie.'

'No,' said Eddie. 'We haven't set up the sequel yet.'

Without warning, the sky turned dark, as a huge shadow appeared overhead. Everyone looked up to see a spacecraft one hundred and twelve times bigger than the *Messenger*. As it descended from the clouds, everyone ran (Sanjay hobbled) from the playground in terror. The Class-G space cruiser, named the *Scanty Shrimp*, came down on top of St Ernie's School. Its enormous weight crushed the building to dust. All the kids cheered.

'I love aliens,' said Eddie.

In the bottom right-hand corner of the spaceship, a tiny door slid open. Liquid steps flowed out and solidified. Down them wiggled a strange creature, made of what looked like millions of pieces of string. It resembled a badly drawn snake. It slithered its way up the now-abandoned platform. It reached up to the mic. Each string in its body vibrated to create sounds, forming into English words.

'Greetings, Earth people. I come from the planet Glugg-glugg, in the Andromeda galaxy. I'm here on behalf of the FFOG – the Football Federation of Galaxies. Your Milky Way has now met the required footballing level and you've been invited to play in the Inter-Galactic Cup, against the other fifteen known footballing galaxies. I am looking for the team Earth United.'

Everyone pointed to Nick, Mia, Phil, Sanjay and Eddie. They in turn pointed to the real Ronaldo, Morgan, Messi, Mbappé and Haaland. Before they had time to react, the real players were quickly stunned, knocked unconscious, and abducted on to the spacecraft.

Without so much as a goodbye, the *Scanty Shrimp* took off and disappeared into the clouds.

Nick watched it leave and felt a tiny bit sad. This was the end of their epic journey. Soon, it would be back to school (once they rebuilt it), and normal life.

Above them, a sonic boom sounded and the clouds turned black.

Phil pointed upwards. 'Why's the spaceship coming back?'

'Maybe they forgot their passports,' said Nick.

'Or need to dump their rubbish,' added Sanjay.

'Maybe time works differently in their galaxy and they're back already,' suggested Mia.

'This is just like that *Avengers* film,' said Eddie. 'Wait, I know . . . "No, it isn't, Eddie" . . . Right, guys?'

The look of terror on everyone's faces told Eddie his answer.

Nick then said the word the team had been dreading. 'Run!'

# EXTRA TIME

In the heart of the Andromeda galaxy, on the planet Kreesh, the real Cristiano Ronaldo looked at the real Lionel Messi and said, 'You think we can win this?'

'Well,' said Messi, 'there's us, Haaland and Morgan, but with Mbappé injured, I'm not too sure about our replacement keeper.'

They both looked down the pitch, towards their own goal. Standing between the sticks, eating a packet of ready salted crisps, was Phil.

'Don't worry,' Phil said, crisps flying from his over-filled mouth. He bent down and pulled a

Flompa Wompa bar (now available on Earth, for a limited time) from his backpack. 'I've got it sorted!'

The whistle blew, and the match between the Real Earth United and the ten-foot-high Goliathans of the Black Eye galaxy began.

# ACKNOWLEDGEMENTS

This book would not exist in any shape or form without my amazing editor, Shalu Vallepur. She championed it from the very beginning and helped to shape and mould the book into what you've read today ('cut for pacing' still haunts my dreams). I can't thank her enough.

I would like to thank everyone at Chicken House (or Floottell House as it's known throughout the galaxy) for taking a chance on a crazy story about football. I'm eternally grateful to Barry, Rachel, Esther and more. If I've missed your name, it's down to pacing (see above).

A shout-out also to Gabrielle Chant for the great suggestions and to Aleksei Bitskoff for the fantastic book cover.

A special mention to Hebburn library and their staff. When my laptop suddenly passed away, your facilities and help saved my bacon. Much appreciated.

To my friend and first reader, John Pounder.

Thank you for your time, patience and ~~crisps~~ wisdom.

For my kids, who not only inspired the idea but encouraged me to send it out into the world. I love you more than ~~words~~ crisps!

To my wife Lisa, who's put up with me for over three decades. Everything I write is for you.

And finally, to you the readers. I hope you enjoyed the world of Nick and his friends as much as I enjoyed writing it. Till the next time, I thank you all.

Alan

P.S. I would like to apologize to Millwall FC. You just rhymed better than Walsall.